Fear in Florence

by
Jean Anderson
&
Linda Lininger

HANNAH & NIKI ADVENTURES SERIES™
INFOHI PUBLISHING

Edited by Joe Lubow

Published in the United States of America by InfoHi Publishing

Design: Sheffield Graphics, Ben Lomond, CA 95005

ISBN 0-9717849-0-6

Printed in the United States of America
InfoHi Publishing
Box 1688
Fremont, CA 94538
831-685-1063
http://www.infohi.com

First Printing, October, 2002

Table of Contents

Dedication

We dedicate this book to
a new understanding of world religions
that will bring peace to the world and to
a clean energy source that will eliminate
our dependence on fossil fuel.

Chapter 1
Vacation in Florence

"**W**hat's that?" Niki asked her best friend Hannah as she leaned across the airplane seat to see the display screen on Hannah's new laptop computer. Not looking where she was leaning, Niki's ice and Coke went flying across her lap and spilled everywhere, just missing the laptop.

"Hey! Look out! I've only had this laptop for a week!" said Hannah, whipping the laptop away from her friend's mess.

WHUMP!

The plane dropped straight downward hard. All the passengers gasped at once as iced drinks and stuff went flying everywhere. Those passengers that were not belted in and several of the flight attendants landed in ungraceful positions as a result of the plane's sudden jolt.

For a few seconds everyone braced themselves for another jolt. Then the flight attendants burst into action helping people into their seats. Fortunately, since the flight had just begun, most of the passengers were still just getting used to being in the air and still had their seat belts on.

A voice came over the public address system. "This is Captain Arnold. We have apparently encountered some unexpected turbulence. Our flight path has been revised, and we are advised by ground control to avoid the storm systems to our south." The captain sounded calm.

Hannah and Niki clung to each other with the laptop between them.

Hannah Jordan and Niki Parker, best friends, were flying to Milan on their way to Florence, Italy, with Hannah's grandmother, Mrs. Boyce. The lucky teenagers were asked by Mrs. Boyce to accompany her to the Florence Wine and Art Show and to tour

Florence, one of the most beautiful cities in the world.

The teens were seated together in the first row of the first-class cabin, and Mrs. Boyce was seated a few rows behind them.

"Hannah! Are you all right?" Hannah could hear a note of alarm in her grandmother's voice.

"I'm fine, Grandma. So is Niki. We're still belted in like we are supposed to be," Hannah reassured her worried grandmother. Hannah could sense her grandmother relax at the sound of her voice and smiled to herself. Her grandmother was always there for her.

"Ladies and gentlemen." The flight attendant took her turn at the microphone. "The captain has turned on the seat belt sign. Everyone, please return to your seats and remain seated with your seat belts fastened."

"Now she tells us," Niki joked.

"Oh, nuts," fifteen-year-old blond Niki sputtered, looking down at her once-perfectly creased tan slacks that matched the stripe in her violet sweater vest.

"You didn't ruin that beautiful cardigan sweater that matches that set, did you?" asked Hannah.

"No, luckily the sweater is up in the overhead compartment!" replied Niki. "Good thing we're traveling with your grandmother, who booked us in first class, or I would have stained the whole row of people with that jolt!" replied Niki, pressing the button for help from the flight attendant.

"When I travel with Dad to Mom's movie sets, we fly coach, and I hate it," she continued. "Daddy is a hippie at heart, and I love him for that, but not when we fly. I need space!"

"You sure do!" said Hannah, taking the towel from the attendant to wipe the soda from the seat tray table.

Holding her new laptop, Hannah said, "I've never asked my grandmother for anything this expensive, but I begged her for this laptop. It rocks! It even has a wireless satellite uplink. I don't need to plug it into a phone line to get to the Internet; it's built-in wireless!"

"I am a mess!" said Niki, brushing her pants and watching the stain spread all down her legs. The attendant took the towels, shook her head, and left for the front of the cabin with a look of impatience.

While Niki fretted over her stained clothes, Hannah logged onto the Internet, opened her email box, and checked for messages. Just the usual "farewell, travel safely" message from her mother, a teasing "drop dead" from her brother Jimmy, and a "don't eat the meat or drink the water" warning from her father. "At least email keeps me in touch with everyone," Hannah said softly as she logged off email and pointed her web browser at Google.com so she could search for information on Florence, Italy.

"Excuse me." The captain's voice sounded apologetic. "Our course change has been accomplished, and we are now in storm-free skies. I will be turning off the seat-belt sign shortly. Please stay seated until then. Thank you for flying to Milan with us today. The weather in Milan today is a balmy 79 degrees with a chance of an afternoon shower. I hope you enjoy the rest of your flight with us today."

Niki fidgeted until the seat-belt sign went off, and when it did she dashed for the first-class restroom to make sure she got there before anyone else. Successful in her effort, she was only gone a minute.

"Anything exciting in cyberspace today?" Niki asked, returning from the restroom dressed in her first emergency outfit. "We haven't been in the air ten minutes, and I'm already in my just-in-case outfit. Good thing I brought two emergency outfits with me in my carry-on." She winked at Hannah as she slid back into her seat and buckled up.

"That turbulence really did my first outfit in," Niki complained.

"If I remember correctly," Hannah teased Niki, "you spilled Coke all over yourself long before we hit any turbulence."

"That is simply…," Niki paused, "the plain, painful truth. I'm a total klutz." Niki smiled and shrugged her shoulders. "What can I do? I was born this way."

Both girls laughed and got back to the business of going on vacation.

"I hope I brought the right clothes," said Hannah, looking at herself and then at Niki. It was hard to look good next to the daughter of a movie star.

"You look wonderful, Hannah." Niki nodded at Hannah reassuringly. "And if we didn't bring the right stuff, we'll just have to go shopping." She grinned and rubbed her hands together.

"Would you ladies care for a refill?" Delia, the middle-aged flight attendant asked, her tray balanced precariously in one hand and a pitcher of ice water in the other.

"None for me," Niki said. "Hasn't she ever heard of turbulence?" she asked Hannah.

"Me, either," Hannah added. "But we'd like two blankets, please. Remember your air-crash disaster training, Niki? We just may need those blankets to protect ourselves from jet-plane fuel if we have to ditch this bird."

"Hannah, you are going to Florence. I hope when we are enraptured with the art and beauty of Florence, you will give the laptop a rest," Mrs. Boyce commented with a laugh as she passed the girls on her way to the restroom. "I'm glad you two were buckled in. That was a pretty big jolt." She grinned at Hannah and patted her shoulder gently.

Mrs. Boyce was dressed in a navy-blue St. John's designer casual and blue pumps, which was anything but casual. Her knit suit was trimmed in white and her matching pillbox hat was flawlessly perched in her beautiful brunette hair with a gray streak at the border and swept back in a sleek twist.

"Oh, hi, Grandma. You know me. I like to be prepared." Hannah pinched her grandmother's arm as she passed.

"Your grandmother is the greatest," Niki whispered to Hannah. "I hope I look that good at her age. I can't believe she invited me to come with you two on this trip. And all first class, too. She is just, just—the best."

In Niki's heart of hearts, she wished that Hannah's grandmother were *her* grandmother. In a word, Mrs. Boyce was perfect. Niki, the only child of James Parker, a San Francisco art dealer, and the film star, Marilyn James, tried to live what she called a "normal" life. Niki never mentioned her mother's identity to anyone, attended a first-rate public school, and preferred to worry about teenage-girl concerns like clothes, boys, and homework rather than get caught up in her mother's celebrity.

Hannah and Niki met ten years ago in the California wine country, where Niki's Aunt Mel and Hannah's grandmother are best friends and next-door neighbors. Every year since then, they've looked forward to spending their summers together.

"I'm not even sure that I asked her to invite you. I think she read my mind." Hannah grinned and turned her attention back to her laptop. "I just wish this trip hadn't come up right at this time. Now I have to write a history paper while we are here to make up for missing the first ten days of school. Mr. Doherty gave me the topic "Muslims in European History." I've never even studied Muslims before. Have you?"

"No. That really stinks," Niki added. "I have a really heavy load this semester. Maybe I can write a paper too—on the same topic—for social studies or something. Problem is we are not studying Europe, but maybe I can think of a tie-in. I have two weeks to think about it. Just make sure you research it really well, and then I can use your stuff and write a different paper. And, I'm not going to think about it right now, okay?"

"My dad works with a lot of different marine biologists. Some of them are Muslim," replied Hannah, continuing anyway. "One guy stayed at our house last year, and he prayed five times a day. He told me that they use some of the books from the

Old Testament in the Bible. I couldn't believe it! Christians trace their history back to Abraham's son, Joseph, and Muslims trace theirs back to Ishmael. It seems that's where the two religions split off."

"One thing I remember from my class last year in world government is that girls our age in Afghanistan have to wear a weird tent thing they call a *burka*. You can't even see that there's a person inside one! A group called the Taliban runs the country, and they don't like females too much." Niki winced.

"Aunt Mel wrote a story about it, too. She interviewed Jay Leno's wife for the story, who has been trying to help them for years. Girls are beaten right in the street for not wearing that *burka* thing. Last week these guys shot a woman in the head for having an affair. Of course, the guy she was with didn't get shot. It is so wrong! I am so glad I was not born in a country like that!" Niki exclaimed.

"I know," said Hannah. "Well, Italy is a nice civilized place. I've saved some maps off the Internet to use in the report. It shouldn't be too bad staying in the art capital of the world." Hannah smiled broadly.

"Hannah." Niki nudged Hannah with her elbow. "Don't look now, but there's a cute guy sitting in the seat across the aisle from me." Niki looked down at the magazine in front of her and quickly glanced across the aisle with her eyes.

Hannah leaned way forward almost touching her computer screen with her forehead and said real loudly, "Who? Where?" Grinning, she sat back up and tilted her head teasingly at Niki.

Niki looked at Hannah with her eyes wide open and in a low voice said, "I am going to use your toothbrush to groom my dog." Then they both burst into laughter. Every passenger in the first-class cabin glowered in their direction. Hannah and Niki could put up quite a cloud of noise without even realizing they were doing it.

"Let me through! Get out of my way!" The tall man from the coach cabin shoved the passengers in the first-class cabin aside rudely as he charged up the aisle. "I want to talk to the captain," he demanded loudly as he tried to push past Delia, who stood her ground in front of him.

"The captain is in the cockpit flying the plane." Delia did not budge.

"This flight change will delay our arrival in Milan by an hour, which is unacceptable," the man raged.

Hannah and Niki looked at each other in silence as they tried to make sure they heard every word the man was saying.

"I want to see the captain now!" the man demanded.

"I will ask the captain to come and see you, but you are not allowed to go into the cockpit uninvited." Delia remained calm in spite of the man's growing agitation.

"Man, are we being hijacked?" Niki asked nervously.

"I hope not," Hannah replied. "If we are, I might have to protect myself by throwing my new laptop at that guy, and I don't want to do that." She frowned.

"Please, sir, return to your seat, and I'll ask the captain to come and talk to you," Delia instructed calmly.

"No. I want to see the captain! Now!" the man exclaimed and tried to rush past Delia.

"No, sir." Delia jumped in front of the man and physically did not allow him to pass.

Hearing the disturbance, the captain appeared at the cockpit door. He looked concerned.

"May I help you, sir?" the captain said politely but with obvious authority.

"Yes, I mean no. I mean . . ." The man stammered and backed down.

"Sir, please return to your seat. Our flight plan has been altered by ground control, and there is nothing we can do about it," the captain said firmly, taking the man by the elbow and leading him back toward his seat.

Delia came over to Hannah and Niki. "Can I get you two anything?" she asked smiling.

"That sure was scary," Niki remarked. "Is everything all right?"

"Yes. No need to be concerned," she reassured them. "We were very lucky. It's at a time like this when I wish we had a sky marshal on the flight. In fact, I think that we need to have a sky marshal on every flight. And every passenger has to be alert. You should always look around you and be prepared for anything," Delia warned. "I think we are okay now. But always be alert." She smiled at them warmly.

"Start watching that plane move across the map. You've got quite a few hours ahead of you. Here is our destination—Milan." She pointed to a huge world map in the front of the cabin with a little plane projected on it. "Here's where we are right now."

"We know, but we have lots of stuff to entertain us. We have to get on a new plane in Milan to get to Florence. It's going to be a long trip," said Hannah. "Thanks for your help."

The in-flight entertainment included the usual news and reruns of syndicated television sitcoms and then a movie. Hannah and Niki settled down to a low roar and entertained themselves with the load of fashion magazines Niki had brought from home. Hannah searched the Internet for interesting information about Florence.

"Hannah, I need to get into my carry-on bag again. I forgot about the sea-mist spray my mother gave me. She says that it is vital for moisturizing while flying. She flies a lot, you know." Niki talked until Hannah looked up.

"I didn't even recognize her in her last movie. The person on the screen is not the mom I know that flies in on Friday night and makes me French toast on

Saturday morning. My mom looks pretty normal on Saturday. And she does know a lot about how to take care of herself. I believe the sea mist is just what the doctor ordered."

Niki got out of her seat after the flight attendant wheeled the beverage cart past her. She opened the overhead compartment, found her carry-on bag, and opened the front zippered pocket. As soon as the pocket was fully opened, its contents tumbled out all at once, catching Niki quite by surprise. Batting at the sweaters and outfit extras that came falling out at her, Niki lost her balance and flopped like a rag doll into the lap of the guy that she had previously referred to as "that cute guy."

Not expecting to have a fifteen-year-old girl fall into his lap, Peter Brown looked up and instinctively caught the falling teenager in his arms and gently lifted her back to her feet.

Niki's face turned a bright red that contrasted nicely with her light-blond hair. Peter blushed, too.

"Why—why are you going to Milan?" Niki blurted.

"I'm traveling to Milan to go to the Fashion Institute there."

"To be surrounded by models?" asked Niki. She couldn't think of anything to say. She was so embarrassed.

"I'm a designer," said Peter with an accent that Niki didn't recognize. "I've observed that modeling can be a very competitive profession that doesn't always bring out the best in people. I'm on a scholarship. What about you?"

Lifting Niki gently back to her feet, Peter looked down at the scattered clothing and makeup and said, "Drop something?"

"Pths," was all Niki managed to say.

"Please forgive my friend Niki here. She's having a blond moment." Hannah leaned over to help steady Niki and pick up her stuff.

"Peter Brown." Peter extended his hand toward Hannah. "Nice to meet you."

"Hannah Jordan," Hannah replied automatically. "Nice to meet you."

Hannah smiled and released Peter's hand just a moment before he released his grip.

Picking up her belongings and stashing them back into her carry-on, Niki felt like the center of too much unwanted attention. She tried to disappear into her seat and looked at the in-flight magazine, trying to figure out what the movie was going to be. "Oh, no," Niki thought to herself. "It's *Dr. Doolittle II*. I've seen it. Too cute and too…"

"Well, blushing Blondie, have you had enough of throwing yourself at men?" Hannah asked Niki jokingly.

"Oh, God. What will happen next?" Niki asked.

"Nothing if you just sit there." Hannah patted Niki's seat. Hannah pointed to the laptop display screen.

"Look at this, Niki." Hannah stared intently at the screen. "The jewelry merchants on the famous Ponte Vecchio—that's a bridge in Florence—are in an uproar. Did you know that Florence means 'abundance' or 'wealth'? Diamonds and diamond jewelry are being stolen right out from under their noses. Security is getting tighter and tighter, but nothing seems to help."

"I love diamonds," said Niki. "They are so romantic. My mother has a spectacular diamond sweetheart

necklace that she got from the *Love at the End* movie.
The producer gave it to her when she was nominated
for the Academy Award. Too bad she didn't win.
Who is stealing the diamonds?" asked Niki.

 "No one knows," replied Hannah. "Some people
think terrorists may be stealing them to fund terrorist
attacks like the one on that ship, the *USS Cole*, last
year. The Florentine police are freaked about it, too.
The article said there will be a huge diamond jewelry
exposition at the wine show that we are going to with
my grandmother at the Palazzo Vecchio. Right on."

 "Isn't the Palazzo Vecchio on the Piazza della
Signoria where we are staying? Cool!" said Niki
without waiting for an answer. "I bet they will have
beautiful diamonds there. Why do they need
diamonds to fund attacks? Why don't they just use
money?"

"I remember a guy in New Jersey getting arrested for
smuggling diamonds for organized crime," replied
Hannah, leaning in to whisper to Niki. "He was a
short squat guy. He bought the diamonds in Jersey
City and took them to Italy where he sold them for
quick cash to pay for a hit on a guy from another
family. Diamonds are small and easy to hide. He had

money to spend in Italy without having to exchange it at a bank, and most diamonds can't be traced," finished Hannah.

Hannah always read the crime page. Starting with reading the Nancy Drew books, she loved trying to figure out who did the crime and, more importantly, why.

"You know, Hannah, in some ways Italy is a very scary place." Niki spoke softly since everyone on the plane was traveling to Italy. "Italy may be a fashion capital, with Versace and all, but there are a lot of really scary criminals, organized crime, terrorist groups, and a bunch of stuff, too. When my mother was there in 1993 shooting a movie in Florence, the Mafia set off a bomb at the Uffizi Gallery right on Signoria Plaza where we'll be staying, and it killed people. My mom had just visited there the day before!"

"Speaking of Versace, let's look at the Milan fashion show Web site. Maybe we can talk your grandmother into letting us go," said Niki. "Maybe my mother can get us some tickets."

"Cool!" said Hannah. She smiled at Niki. "The best thing that ever happened to me was Niki moving in next door to me for the summer ten years ago," thought Hannah. "Besides being her best friend who she could tell anything to, she had cool parents. Hannah's parents were nerd scientists and divorced. Niki's mother was a famous movie star, and her father was an artist with a successful gallery in San Francisco; and they were still in love."

Hannah connected to the Internet using her laptop. "Here's an email from my brother Jimmy's college roommate, Brian. He is so cool."

"I remember him," said Niki. "I met him up at your grandmother's house in Calistoga. He's a hunk and too old for you. What is he writing you for?"

"He just wants me to know that he loves me and wants to be with me forever," said Hannah, turning to look at Niki's shocked face.

"Just kidding! I got you that time," said Hannah laughing. "He is a stock trader. Let's wave to him in the World Trade Center when we fly over it. He works for Cantor Fitzgerald on one of the top floors. I got the full tour when I went to see my mother in New York last time. He is *so* nice. He is the nicest of my brother's friends, and when I'm in my twenties, our age difference won't matter!"

"I hope you fall in love before your twenties!" replied Niki horrified.

"Don't get so serious on me, Blondie," said Hannah. "Brian is nice—that's it. Sometimes I like to dream about him. I'm going to email him that we are waving to him now." Hannah pushed Send and turned to Niki.

"What is the name of the fashion show? I'll find the Web site," said Hannah, bringing up Google.com on the laptop to do the search.

"Try 'Milan Fall Fashion Festival,'" said Niki peering at the laptop screen. "This is so cool that we can get to the Internet up here! Let's bring up the Web site!" Niki felt a tap on her shoulder and jumped up, hitting her head on the overhead.

"Ouch!" she said, looking up.

It was Peter Brown. "How embarrassing," thought Niki.

"Are you girls going to the fashion shows in Milan?" asked Peter. "I see you've got the Web site up on your screen there." He motioned toward the laptop that was now on Niki's lap. "Are you two models?"

"Oh, no. Not us. I mean, definitely not me," Hannah sputtered. "We're going to Florence to the Wine and Art Festival. My grandmother is going to the winery show to buy vines to plant in her vineyard in Calistoga, California. She wants to make more winning wines using the California climate and Italian vines," Hannah explained.

"Well, if you should get to Milan, the shows are going to be on for an entire week. I only have tickets to one show, but I hope to find some seats available to students. My classes don't start until next week, but I am getting there early just for this," Peter went on.

"Modeling, psst," Niki interjected. "Too much makeup! Clothes are too tight and too weird. They stick you with pins, tape up stuff that should never be taped up, put goo on your teeth, spray ice water on you, blow huge fans at you, and make you wear three-inch spike heels. 'Now walk, smile, or don't,' depending on how weird the clothes are and 'Don't trip, fall down, or laugh.' Yuck, I'd rather be a veterinarian."

"Don't pay any attention to her. She's just sour grapes because God made her beautiful," Hannah said, teasing Niki.

"Beauty has nothing to do with modeling on a runway," replied Niki. "If you're a model, they think of you as a hanger with feet. If the hanger is too plump, too short, too tall, too smart, too whiny, too whatever, it's out. There are always a zillion other hangers."

"Well, I'm not a model. I'm a designer. I mean, I will be a designer," Peter smiled. "I've got a part-time job in Milan, too, giving tours of the city. Are you all going to spend any time there?"

"Oh, no," Hannah blurted out. "We're just making a plane change at the airport, and then it's off to Florence.

"Too bad." Peter eyed Hannah and smiled. "I would love to show you the city. It has some fabulous things to see. I'm really looking forward to going to a few of the shows and earning some big money giving tours to the ritzy crowd that comes to these shows. I'm stationed at one of the best hotels in Milan."

Hannah and Niki both thought almost out loud that Peter was really cute with his tussled, artistic look. His brown khaki pants and blue button-down shirt were neat and well coordinated with a brown leather belt, brown loafers, and a creamy soft, off-white cashmere

v-necked vest. During the rest of the flight, Niki
often caught him looking at Hannah.

Both Hannah and Niki dozed off during *Dr. Doolittle
II*. The beverage cart woke them both up as Delia
made her final round of the first-class cabin.

Hannah and Niki said good-bye to Peter as they
deplaned and got on the bus to ride to the Milan
terminal. After a short ride, Hannah, Niki, and Mrs.
Boyce approached the transfer desk. Handing the
tickets to the agent at the transfer desk, all three of
the travelers looked a little bit tired; they felt like they
could use some real rest.

"I'm sorry, *Signora*." The agent spoke in English.
"You do not have a reservation on the flight to
Florence."

"But, you have our confirmed tickets in your hand,"
Mrs. Boyce protested.

"Yes, *Signora*, you have tickets, but you do not have a
reservation on the flight."

"Please call your supervisor," Mrs. Boyce said
sternly.

"Yes, *Signora*," the agent said as he got up and walked to the other end of the counter.

A woman with a badge that said she was the supervisor came to the counter where Mrs. Boyce was standing and said, "Yes, *Signora*, Antonio is correct. You have tickets, but you do not have a reservation on the flight. The flight appears to be full, and you must go to the standby counter and wait there."

"Wait for what?" Mrs. Boyce demanded.

"A standby seat," the supervisor answered.

"A standby seat?" Mrs. Boyce's voice was getting higher and higher.

"Yes, up the stairs, through the passport check. Take a left, go to the end of the hall and take another left. Go down the stairs, and you are there." She handed the tickets back to Mrs. Boyce, and off the travelers went. Fortunately the luggage had been shipped in advance, so all they had to do was cope with their carry-on bags.

After following the directions and making a stop at the information counter, the travelers finally ended up at the standby counter with about a hundred other people, many of whom Hannah and Niki recognized as their fellow Continental Airlines passengers from the earlier flight.

"So, it looks like there's monkey business going on with this standby thing," Hannah said as they waited in line.

"Didn't you read something about organized crime in Italy?" Niki asked.

"Yes, but Continental Airlines is an American-based company," Hannah said.

When they got to the head of the line, the counter agent snatched the tickets that Mrs. Boyce handed to her and jammed them on the top of a huge pile of other people's tickets.

"But, but . . . those are our tickets!" protested Mrs. Boyce as the counter agent brushed her aside and said the Italian equivalent of "next."

"Well, this will never do," Hannah heard her grandmother mumble under her breath.

"Let's go, girls. I have an idea or two." Mrs. Boyce grabbed her carry-on bag and headed back down the hallway they had come from. "I saw the Captain's

Club as we passed it, and I'm going to see if there's any way to cut through this Italian red tape."

The girls followed Mrs. Boyce as closely as they could, but they were amazed how a woman of her age could move so fast. "She's a wonder," Niki thought to herself.

Entering the Captain's Club, the three travelers were met by two uniformed agents sitting at the front desk.

"*Ciao*. Good morning." The first agent greeted them, smiling. "How can I help you?"

For the next twenty minutes, Hannah and Niki watched in wonder as Mrs. Boyce quizzed the agent about possible alternative ways to get to Florence, about buying new tickets, about flight availability, and about their ticket situation. The agent typed and typed, calling up screen after screen of information neither girl could read.

Finally, after three phone calls, the agent said to Mrs. Boyce, "Take your girls and head to the standby desk right now. They are going to call the standby passengers in five minutes. Make sure you are standing near the counter. Go now. *Ciao*. Have fun in

Florence." The agent smiled and waved as they left the Captain's Club.

"I think she may have pulled a few strings for us," Mrs. Boyce said as they rushed down the hall. "Italy is a country of privilege. You have to work the system over here. You two will figure it out soon enough. You are smart. Just watch me." She smiled and continued down the hallway to the standby counter.

"Boyce!" The standby counter agent called just as they arrived.

"That's me," Mrs. Boyce said, as she took the three tickets from the agent's hand. "*Grazie.*"

Within ten minutes the three travelers were on the transfer bus to the Air Italia plane sitting on the tarmac in front of them.

"One more takeoff and landing, and we're in Florence," Hannah said with excitement.

"I can't wait," Niki added. "I'm hungry."

Chapter 2
Arriving in Florence

inally, the plane landed in Florence, and Hannah and Niki noticed the Italian military jeeps on the side of the tarmac. "I wonder what that's all about?" Hannah asked Niki.

"Who knows?" Niki said, trying not to stare at the beautifully dressed woman standing next to her.

"Will our luggage be there, Grandma?" asked Niki.

"Our luggage will be there, waiting for us. The cab driver has instructions on where to pick it up." Mrs. Boyce smiled at Niki fondly. "I arranged for our suitcases to be shipped to our apartment about a week before we left. Getting through customs with a huge suitcase can take a long time, especially in Italy,"

Mrs. Boyce continued. "Because we don't have luggage, we can avoid all of that fuss in customs and go directly to meet our driver."

"Pretty smart," Niki smiled back at Mrs. Boyce.

Once inside the terminal, the rest of the passengers headed for the baggage-claim area.

"Hannah and Niki, follow me," Mrs. Boyce commanded as she headed for the exit to meet their driver. Just then, a huge bang rang through the terminal building.

Everyone, including Mrs. Boyce, dropped to the floor and put their hands over their heads.

Hannah landed right on top of her carry-on case and rolled off to land right on top of Niki. Both girls were too frightened to laugh at how silly they looked lying in a heap on the floor. Everyone looked around to locate the source of the explosion.

The only person who didn't react to the sound was the guard next to the door.

After she gathered her composure, and noticing that the guard was unaffected, Mrs. Boyce asked, "What was that?"

"Just another abandoned suitcase. Beware, if you leave your suitcase unattended, the police will pick it up. The one they just found looked suspicious, so it was neutralized. We have many threats, but I think the police . . . they like the explosions." The guard shrugged.

"Your English is very good," Mrs. Boyce complimented the guard.

"Thank you, *Signora*. You are very kind to notice. I am studying to be a teacher," he replied.

"Well, I wish you well." Mrs. Boyce smiled and motioned to the girls that they should get up and move out of the way. By then everyone was slowly getting up and mumbling to each other. .

"They ought to warn us if they are going to blow something up," Niki complained as they exited the terminal door.

"Mrs. Boyce!" said a short man with a New York Yankees baseball cap and a thick Italian accent walking briskly toward them. "I'm Sr. Cardini, your driver!" He pointed to a black Volvo station wagon parked illegally at the curb.

Hannah bolted toward Cardini's cab and peered through the windows. "Hurray!" Hannah exclaimed. "I can see our suitcases in the car!"

"I was just too afraid to look." Niki mugged a sullen face. Then she cracked up and smiled broadly. "We're actually here!" she shouted for the world to hear.

Niki felt really tired after the long trip, but excitement was replacing her fatigue. Hannah was already in the car and looking out the window expectantly after verifying that the luggage was all there.

Cardini was obviously very familiar with the city of Florence. He drove right past the sign that looked like it said "no cars." They wound through tiny streets and alleys for what seemed like an hour. Hannah and Niki looked at each other with alarm. Cardini made very little effort to stop to let pedestrians walk across the street. It was a very busy place and very crowded, with groups of tourists following umbrella-waving tour guides.

"Here we are! The Piazza Della Signoria. Home of the great Medici family. That is their palace right next to your apartment!" said Sr. Cardini with a flourish. Cardini drove right down the middle of it.

"Look, girls—the replica of the statue of David!" said Mrs. Boyce. Sr. Cardini slowed down slightly for them to look.

The girls stared at the statue of the naked young man. You could see *every*thing.

Hannah and Niki looked at each other and grinned.

"Look at the horse-drawn carts! Grandma," Hannah said as she tapped on her grandmother's shoulder when they passed the horses, "let's take a ride around the city in one of those buggies. It would be a blast."

"I was just thinking that myself," Mrs. Boyce said, smiling at Hannah.

"Look, Niki, that horse looks a lot like Bounty." Hannah chirped with excitement about her horse that her grandmother kept on the ranch in Calistoga for her.

"Where's our apartment?" Niki asked as they all looked around trying to find it.

Just then, Cardini stopped the cab and jumped out. He shouted something in Italian that sounded mean to the man standing in front of the alley and then got back into the cab. The man moved about two feet and shot Cardini a mean look. Cardini moved the cab ten feet down the alley. He pointed at the door to the first building.

"I think this is it," Mrs. Boyce said as she looked at the receipt from the rental agency. "This says to push the button next to 'Francesco,' and the owner, Eduardo, will be there to greet us and give us the keys."

Hannah read down the list of names next to the doorbells, and Francesco was right there on the list. She pushed the doorbell button and heard a buzzer sound upstairs.

A young man's voice answered the bell. "I'll come down to show you up."

"Hmmm . . . sounds cute," Niki thought as she looked down at her crumpled shirt and khaki slacks. "I look like a mess." She reached into her purse for her hairbrush. Two seconds later, her blond hair was neatly brushed rather than a tangled mess.

Hannah was too busy trying to look into the covered windows to pay any attention to her hair.

Mrs. Boyce gently nudged the girls out of the way and greeted Eduardo when he opened the front door.

Both girls gasped involuntarily as Eduardo stepped through the door to take Mrs. Boyce's hand.

Eduardo was dressed in the typical Italian style, all black. His shoulder-length jet-black hair was neatly tied back at his neckline, but a few strands had escaped to hang in loose waves around his angular face. Long black eyelashes accented his deep brown eyes. He was, in a word, a hunk.

"It is a pleasure to meet you, *Signora*," Eduardo greeted Mrs. Boyce.

Reluctantly releasing his hand, Mrs. Boyce turned to Hannah and Niki and said, "This is my granddaughter, Hannah, and her best friend, Niki. They've come to keep me company and to learn a little bit about art and Italian history. This is the richest city in the world for art and culture."

"Niki," Hannah elbowed Niki in the ribs, "stop drooling."

"I am not drooling," Niki protested. "You stop staring. Your eyeballs are going to get all sunburned if they pop out any further."

"I am perfectly under control. See?" Hannah said as she grinned and stood on one foot.

Both girls laughed as Mrs. Boyce and Eduardo turned to go into the apartment house.

As they entered the dark entry hall, Eduardo began the guided tour.

"This building has been standing in this location for over five hundred years," Eduardo said as they rounded the first set of spiral steps. "There is an elevator, but as you can see it is quite small."

The elevator ran up the center of the staircase. It was a tiny metal cage that didn't look like it would be able to hold more than one person.

"I'll go down and help Cardini put the luggage in the lift in a minute," said Eduardo as he reached the door to the apartment.

"The lock is kind of complicated. You first turn the lock two revolutions to the right. Then take the key and turn it four revolutions to the left." Eduardo demonstrated. Hannah hoped Grandma was paying attention because it looked hard.

The travelers all strained to see as the door swung open to reveal an ornate entry that led to a spectacular sitting room overlooking the magnificent plaza. The massive windows were arched and had inner and outer shutters. A soft white-lace curtain hung over the window sill and fluttered in and out as the warm September breeze blew delicious aromas from the restaurants on the plaza below into the apartment.

"You will spend many wonderful moments here above the Plaza," said Eduardo warmly.

"May I present the kitchen, and these doors lead to the shower room and powder room," he continued.

"Our building has been remodeled many times since my family acquired it in the fifteenth century. My father just replaced all the plumbing because the people caused a fire that burned out their apartment. This apartment was spared fire damage, but there was some water damage, so you will be happy to know we have the most modern plumbing on the plaza."

"I get nervous when people start bragging about plumbing," whispered Hannah to Niki. "I mean, shouldn't we be able to count on running water and reliable flushing?"

"This first room is now a bedroom, but it used to be a dentist's office." The room was on the end of the apartment, next to an alley. There were two huge arched windows. One window faced the alley, but the other faced the Piazza Della Signoria.

"What a fabulous view," said Niki excitedly.

Hannah and Niki dashed to the open window and hung over the sill.

"You can see so much from right here. It's beautiful!" both girls exclaimed.

"What's that?" asked Hannah pointing at the tower of the Palazzo Vecchio. "It's so beautiful. It's glowing golden against the sky."

"That's the Palazzo Vecchio, home to the Medicis, the great patrons of the arts," replied Eduardo. "The Wine and Art Festival is being set up in there right now. Have you heard the news about all of our missing diamonds?"

The girls nodded as they hung out of the window to get a full view of the activity below. The early evening crowds were milling about in the plaza. The restaurants were busily serving customers as the horse-drawn buggies plodded rhythmically past their tables.

Eagerly the girls and Mrs. Boyce moved on through the apartment.

The second room was a lovely living room with several comfortable sofas and small tables. This room had Italian scenes painted right on the walls.

"Although my mother is a math teacher, she really wanted to be an artist," said Eduardo. "My grandmother insisted that she study math and science and refused to allow my mother to follow her artistic urges. So my mother uses this apartment as her canvas. These paintings are copies of the masters," said Eduardo pointing to a vineyard scene and a gentle garden scene with stone benches.

The third and fourth rooms were each more beautiful than the first two. The master bedroom had a sumptuous canopy painted next to the bed. At first it actually looked three-dimensional. The last bedroom had a wardrobe closet that was ornately painted and spanned nearly the entire wall.

"Girls." Mrs. Boyce tapped them both on the shoulders to get their attention. "I'm going to sleep in the master bedroom. You two can share the other bedroom with the twin beds. I'll finish up the paperwork with Eduardo, and I think it would be best if we all got a little rest before we have a look around."

"Oh, Grandma. Let's just go now. I'm too excited to rest," said Hannah.

"Well, we are hungry, and I expect we will need to turn in early tonight. But you do look a little bit like an unmade bed, my dear," replied Grandma.

Hannah glanced down at her crumpled outfit and cringed. "Maybe a quick meal, nap, and a shower wasn't a bad idea," she thought to herself, and plopped down on one of the beds.

Eduardo turned to the girls and flashed a gorgeous smile in their direction. "My father had his dentist office in these rooms up until about ten years ago. My grandfather had his practice here before then, and my great-grandfather before him. My ancestors were dentists to the Medici family five hundred years ago. My father wants me to finish my studies and become a dentist just like him."

"Are you in dental school now, Eduardo?" Mrs. Boyce asked.

"I'm in my last year of medical school. I'm studying right now, and classes start again in November. After this year I'll have to pick my specialty. I would rather be a doctor for children, a . . . a . . ."

"A pediatrician?" Niki asked.

"Yes, I think that's what you call them in America. I love babies," Eduardo grinned boyishly.

"Okay, he's perfect," Hannah admitted quietly to Niki.

"I'll leave you ladies for now. If you need me, just call this number." Eduardo wrote his number on a piece of paper and handed it to Mrs. Boyce. "If I don't hear from you before then, I'll pick you up tomorrow."

Eduardo headed toward the door. As he left, he smiled again and closed the door.

Before Hannah and Niki got too carried away with swooning over Eduardo, Mrs. Boyce had them busily getting settled into their rooms. Hannah chose the bed near the huge wardrobe closet, and Niki settled into the bed next to the two arched windows.

Mrs. Boyce didn't need to encourage them to hurry and get ready. Everyone was hungry, and the smell of pizza wafted through the windows.

"Man, am I starved," Niki announced as she charged toward the apartment door.

"With you, Niki," Hannah agreed. "I know the direct way to your heart is through your stomach. You are about to have a wonderful experience. There's no place better in the world to find great food than Italy. You will love it here."

The three weary travelers enjoyed a wonderful Marguerite pizza at the café just below their apartment window.

"This Marguerite pizza, with the cheese and tomato sauce on this thin and crunchy crust, is delicious," said Hannah.

"I agree," said Niki.

They talked about the activities for tomorrow and enjoyed the activity in the plaza until they all agreed that they'd better get some real rest.

Yawning as they wound their way up the spiral steps to the apartment, Hannah nudged Niki. "Did you give that Peter Brown your address?" Hannah teased.

"I certainly did not!" Niki protested.

"Well, I thought for sure he was going to ask you to go steady." Hannah raced up the steps in front of Niki.

"I am too tired to chase you. And that's lucky for you. As I recall, you were the one head-to-head with hunky Eduardo," Niki smiled. "You know, Hannah, this is already a fun trip!"

In only a few minutes, Hannah and Niki were all showered, brushed, and sound asleep.

Mrs. Boyce sipped a cup of tea and wrote a few lines in her travel journal before she said her nightly prayers and turned out the light. Her dream of sharing the fantastic artistic legacy of Florence with Hannah was really happening, and she was very happy.

Chapter 3
Winery Show at Palazzo Vecchio

*R*ays of morning sunlight filtered through the wooden shutter slats and passed across Hannah's eyelids to nudge her awake. Now strange echoing *clop–clop-clop* sounds woke her up. Hannah looked around sleepily. "That's right," she thought. "I'm in Italy." She slid out of bed and opened the huge exterior shutter. The strong smell of the dark Italian coffee drifted up from the coffee-vendor stand in the plaza below.

As Hannah folded her arms around her to brace against a cool upsweep of air, a horse pulling an art-vendor cart, clop-clopped up onto the cobblestone plaza from its nightly storage location on a nearby side street. Cars were not allowed in the plaza without permits, so the horses still pulled their heavy carts onto the plaza just like they did five hundred years ago. After the cart was set up for the day, the horses pulled carriages to trot sightseeing tourists through the streets of Florence, because only cars with special permits were allowed there, too.

"Florence is a walking city without cars," thought Hannah. "My kind of place."

Hannah pushed the windows and shutters wider and studied the copies of the statues *David* and *Neptune's Fountain* in the middle of the plaza. "This place rocks," Hannah thought. Her every fiber was filled with excitement. The last time she was here, she had been too young to appreciate the creative power packed into this city. Not this time.

Hannah planned to fill her journal with details for the history paper. If she wrote a good one, not only would it make up for the missed school days, it could look great on her college applications. College was a beckoning beacon of hope since her parents' divorce. She would create her own happy life, and a good college was part of the plan.

Niki strolled into the room, pulling her wet hair up into a clip. "You're just getting up?" asked Niki impatiently.

"I can't believe you've already showered! I thought you were under that pile of blankets!" wailed Hannah. "Is Grandma up, too?"

"You got it! Get going!" encouraged Niki.

Hannah quickly grabbed some clothes and a towel. "Hi, Grandma," she yelled into the kitchen as she dashed into the bathroom. "I'll be quick!"

"Hi, honey. I won't plan on it. Your breakfast will be ready when you are ready," said Mrs. Boyce with a smile. She loved Hannah with all of her heart.

After her shower, Hannah pulled the terry-cloth bathrobe around her and waltzed into the living room overlooking the plaza, her previous frenzy forgotten. "That coffee smells great!"

"Your lucky aura continues. It turns out that it did not matter that you took forty-five minutes in the bathroom," replied Niki. "Your grandmother had to go down and buy a coffeemaker. We can't figure out that steel thing in the cabinet. I love looking down on this plaza! It's like a movie! Tourists, vendors, bankers, beggars, musicians—it has everyone—and horses, too!"

"And those statues," agreed Hannah. "I can't decide if I like *Neptune's Fountain* or the *David* better. Who could believe that they would have replicas of the magnificent fifteenth-century statues by Michelangelo right out on the plaza? I'm going to add another paper for extra credit. It's going to be easy to write a history paper on this place!"

"And cool, too," said Niki. "Let's get any history thing we can on CDs and look for books, too!"

"Good idea, Niki. We can credit the sources in the footnotes and the bibliography. Working as a team will save us a lot of time and make the papers more interesting, too! I'm going to focus on Michelangelo and his impact on the city of Florence. I love his sculptures, and it will be fun to learn more about him. I've already researched the historical aspect of Florence on the Internet. If I add in some pictures to prove I was here, I should be in good shape. Great idea!"

Scanning Hannah from head to toe, Niki said, "That blue shirt brings out your dark brown eyes, Hannah. That's a good color for you!" Now that she was out of that T-shirt uniform, Hannah was looking really good. With Niki's movie-star mother's expert coaching, Niki's natural flair for style was already developed, and Niki was happy to share with her best friend. It was cool how they each had talents that the other did not and how both liked to have fun.

"Thanks, Niki. I love those Capri's. We look okay for the wine show at the Palazzo Vecchio and to hang out with our new boyfriend, Eduardo," sighed Hannah. "Haven't we learned our lesson after fighting over Geronimo in Calistoga?"

"I hope so, but a little harmless flirting never hurt anything," said Niki. "Maybe we can have a bet on who gets more of his attention."

"Girls, girls! Is that a good way to occupy your mind in one of the most beautiful and exciting places in the world?" interrupted Mrs. Boyce. She swept into the living room. Her peach-colored linen pantsuit with her hair swept up into a French twist gave her an aristocratic air. "Do I look like a duchess?" she asked the girls. "I want to convey that California vintners are as sophisticated as the Italians. After all, we have the better Chardonnay," she said with a smile. California and Italian wineries were always amicable rivals at these wine shows, and Grandma produced award-winning California Chardonnay at her ranch.

Ding Dong!

"Eduardo is here to escort us to the wine show," said Mrs. Boyce. "I can't wait to see the new wines for this year!"

"I can't wait to see Eduardo," said Niki, mischievously buttoning her matching jacket and applying lip gloss as she stood in front of the hallway mirror.

"Starts with a 'b' and rhymes with witch," shouted Hannah as she darted into her bedroom to get her shoes and jacket.

For this trip, Hannah had allowed her grandmother to buy her some matching outfits so she did not have to hassle with figuring out what to wear each day. Between her grandmother and Niki, it was depressing sometimes. She was not a natural clotheshorse and was beginning to accept it. After seeing some pretty poor pictures of herself, she figured that she would just wear the latest styles that Grandma selected for her. Hannah checked herself in the mirror. She had to agree; she looked a lot better now with these clothes, than she did in her usual sloppy T-shirt and baggy pants uniform. "I am lucky to have Grandma," she thought for the millionth time.

"Let's go!" shouted Niki as she opened the door. Hannah pushed past her, and they raced down the circular cement stairs to the first floor, giggling and laughing.

"Wow!" Eduardo stated in his sensual Italian accent as they burst through the outside door to join Mrs. Boyce and Eduardo. "I will be the envy of all the guys at this show! Three beauties, all to myself!"

"You're a shameless flatterer, but I love it," said Mrs. Boyce as she slipped her arm under Eduardo's. "It is gallant of you to escort us."

"I wouldn't think of letting a stranger take you and the girls to this event, *Signora* Boyce. It is my pleasure," said Eduardo. And then to Hannah, "Why do you have such a huge bag, Hannah? What do you have in there?"

"It's my laptop," said Hannah. "Niki and I are missing a cool sleep-over party with friends in Calistoga, and we're going to instant-message our friends who are attending the party while we are here at the winery party. They're getting up especially to email us. It should be about 5:00 AM California time."

"I thought you two didn't live near each other," said Eduardo.

"We don't, but each summer we both stay in Calistoga, California, in the wine country," said Hannah. "I stay with my grandmother, and Niki stays with her aunt, Mel."

"Don't look so confused, Eduardo," she continued. "I love this thing. This laptop has a satellite uplink. I charged the batteries, and I don't need a phone line! And this way we don't miss the party at home."

"I'm competing with a computer?" said Eduardo to Mrs. Boyce in mock horror. "This will be a new one for me. I beg you, ladies, please wait until I've made my introductions and impressed everyone before you ditch me for the PC."

"The Palazzo Vecchio buildings could be in a Thomas Kincaid painting! Gosh, my father the art dealer would gag if he could hear me say that!" said Niki.

A valet in formal wear with red tails greeted them with a flourish. "Welcome," he said with a thick Italian accent.

Eduardo escorted Mrs. Boyce up the grand stairway. Niki and Hannah followed close behind. They stepped into a grand marble foyer with frescoes painted in the domed ceiling. Eduardo handed the invitation to the greeters, and a greeter stepped up to a microphone.

"Announcing *Signora* Hannah Boyce of Second Rising Winery and her guests, Hannah Jordan and Niki Parker."

They started down the steps into a huge gathering hall lined with mahogany tables and winery representatives seated at each one. A massive yellow-and-orange sign, "Welcome to the annual Florence Wine and Art Show," was strung across the room. The multicolored flags from all of the Tuscany towns—Siena, Assisi, and Florence—were set up in the appropriate sections.

In the center of the room was the ornate, marble wine-tasting station. Sculptures of angels and royalty rose up from the marble sinks. The judges tasted the wines here and proclaimed the winners for the year.

Mrs. Boyce was not entering her wines this year; she was just here to buy vines from the winners.

"This is fabulous!" exclaimed Mrs. Boyce.

"This place was owned by the Medici family," said Eduardo. "There are paintings here by Michelangelo, and one of the buildings was designed by Brunelleschi, who designed the Duomo. I will give you the full tour."

Just then a dark handsome man in an expertly tailored suit stepped up to greet them. "Welcome to the Florence Wine and Art Show," he said, taking Mrs. Boyce's hand and kissing it. "I'm Tony Vasari."

"Thank you," said Mrs. Boyce, but she stepped back a bit. Eduardo moved between the girls and Tony.

"*Bon giorno*, Tony. This is Mrs. Boyce's granddaughter, Hannah, and her friend, Niki. They are with me."

"You are a lucky man, Eduardo. Fine, I won't interfere. I want you girls to know if you need anything, just ask me." Tony glowered back at Eduardo, turned, and departed.

"As if his real name is Tony," muttered Eduardo. "His family and other rich Middle Eastern families are trying to buy up all the wineries here. They think they look like us and will just blend in. They've bought up wineries here that have been in the same families for centuries. They've been trying to defeat us with armies since the time of Christ, and now they are buying us with oil money." Eduardo's tone grew cold.

"Wow, that sounds like a long time to hold a grudge. Is there a place with good reception here?" asked Hannah, trying to change the subject.

"Our electricity may not match up, and the phone lines are no good," said Tony, coming up behind them.

"We don't need either of those," replied Niki. "This laptop has lithium batteries and a satellite uplink! We just need a clearing without trees and not under marble."

"I see. Quite modern, aren't you, and girls, too!" Tony pointed to a garden visible through the window. "The west gardens should meet your requirements. *Bon giorno.* Remember, you can count on me if you need anything."

"They won't. Thanks, Tony," said Eduardo firmly.

"He's a cute Italian," whispered Niki as Tony descended the stairs.

"Cute? Italian? Can't you tell the difference between an Italian and an Arab?" asked Eduardo. "He has lots of oil money and no class. His father bought the Ricci family winery and then sent his son over to throw his weight around! Rumors follow Tony around weekly about his conquests of the local Italian girls. He does not follow the strict rules about sex that exist in his country. He is very smooth. Please, girls, I beg you. Stay away from him."

"Sorry, he seems nice. Everyone is nice here," Niki said, feeling stupid. "Why did I say that?" she thought, embarrassed.

"How can you tell an Italian from an Arab?" asked Hannah, defending her friend.

"Italians have better noses and are bronzed, not tan from the desert," replied Eduardo. "Eight hundred thousand Arabs have entered the country in the last ten years. They are running from the violent chaos in their own countries and settling here. Most are good, but we are afraid that some are terrorists and that they have hooked up with our own criminals. Please, meet me in a half-hour after you message, as you call it."

"Wow—that was radical," said Niki. "I wonder why he hates Tony so much?"

The teens entered the gardens, sat down on the wall, and Hannah began to open her laptop case.

"That is an impressive laptop," said Tony, suddenly appearing again and sitting down next to them.

"Thanks!" said Hannah.

"Let me help you," said Tony as Hannah struggled to get the laptop out of the case.

"This is a specially made case. It is made of a new prototype fabric," said Hannah. "You can't see through it with the airport X-ray machines, so I had to take it out of the case and put it through. It's great, though, because it protects the laptop from the sun. That is how I ruined my last laptop. I left it out in the sun, and it never worked again."

"Really? I haven't heard of that material," replied Tony. Tony reached in and lifted out the laptop.

"Thanks, Tony," said Hannah distractedly. Tony placed the laptop on his lap and examined the case.

"Okay, Hannah, log on," said Niki. "This is too cool. This will be the first time we've missed the Autumn in Calistoga party since we were five years old! Geronimo is even coming back for the festival this year. When we're done, I want to go over and see the diamonds, okay?" Hannah nodded and concentrated on the laptop screen.

"Look, here's an email addressed to both of us!"

Hannah opened the email.

```
Hi teen detectives,

Gerry here. Kari and Terry
said you were going to log
on, so I had to come over at
the crack of dawn to say hi.
How are you two beautiful
girls doing? I miss you. The
party was not the same
without you.
```

"I can't believe it!" said Hannah excitedly.

"I *don't* believe it," said Niki, who turned the laptop to face her, pressed Reply, and began to type her reply quickly.

```
Gerry, Aunt Mel told me that
your father was taking you to
```

> Doris Loren's art show in San
> Francisco after the party
> last night and staying in his
> townhouse. How can you be in
> two places at once?

> Ha Ha. LOL,

came back on an instant message to Hannah.

> It's me, Kari, and Terry.

Hannah and Kari typed back and forth.

To Kari:

> U think u r soooo funny. What
> happened at the party?

From Kari:

> Gerry wore white shirt, white
> teeth, and dazzling smile!

was the reply.

To Kari:

> Was he with anyone?

> And don't lie. Remember it
> was us who figured out that
> Mr. Brannan was his father.

From Kari:

```
He was with Rosa, of course.
All recovered from being
pushed off the mountain and
more beautiful than ever. How
is Italy?
```

"Tony, what are you still doing here?" asked Eduardo, strolling into the garden.

Tony got up quickly and handed the case back to Hannah. "I was helping these beautiful girls with their fancy computer. Girls, when do you leave?"

"We're leaving September 16th," said Niki.

"So soon? We Italians will not get to see enough of you!" said Tony, taking Niki's hand and giving it a quick kiss.

"How sweet!" said Niki.

"Girls! Girls! Please let me introduce you to some Italians. Enough on that computer!" persuaded Eduardo.

"Okay," said Hannah.

Hannah typed a goodbye, logged off, snapped the laptop shut, and started to put it in the case again. "Okay," she said, hopping up. "Is there someplace I can stash this?" asked Hannah.

"I don't know," said Eduardo. "I'll ask a friend who has an office in the winery consortium suite of offices downstairs."

"Why wait? I'll store it for you," said Tony coming up behind them.

"Where would you put it?" said Hannah.

"Our company has an office right downstairs with the winery consortium," said Tony.

"Okay," said Hannah. "That will be a lot quicker than going back to the apartment."

"Sure, come with me," said Tony, giving Hannah his arm. "If we don't return in five minutes, Eduardo, you can come investigate."

"I will," insisted Eduardo.

"Meet us inside," said Niki. "Five minutes."

"Okay," said Hannah over her shoulder as she started down the ornate hallway lined with brightly covered frescoes depicting Mary, Joseph, and Jesus.

They stepped down the marble steps with red carpet down the middle. They entered a long hallway with offices on both sides. Tony pushed open a carved mahogany door into a large reception area. A beautiful Italian twenty-something girl greeted them.

"Mr. Vasari, how nice to see you. How can I help you?"

"Please store this young lady's computer in my office."

"Yes, sir," said the woman, taking the laptop.

"Did you know that you are staying in the flat of the former dentist to the Medicis?" asked Tony. "I've heard that there is a ghost there. They say that an unfaithful ancestor of Eduardo's was killed by his wife in the first bedroom there that used to be the dentist's office. Legend has it that the murdered husband gets restless before a tragedy and flaps the windows open. Centuries ago, the night before battles, the soldiers of Florence would gather below in the plaza to see if the windows flapped. When they did, they lost the battle. I would love to see the inside. Have they been opening by themselves this week?" he asked.

"No, not since we've been here, Mr. Vasari." said Hannah.

"Tony, please!" replied Tony. "I'm too young to be called Mr. Vasari by a beautiful young woman such as you. In my country, you would be married already. Do you know that I am related to the Vasari that painted the walls you just saw inside the Palazzo Vecchio? My Muslim ancestors were on a diplomatic mission in Genoa, and one married Vasari's daughter. So I am part Italian."

"Wow, I didn't realize that anyone but Italians lived here," said Hannah as they walked back to the displays in the main hall.

"Well, before 1918, Muslims ruled a large area of the world. Their empire was known as the Ottoman Empire. Have you studied it at school?"

"No," said Hannah. "Not yet. But I am writing a paper on Muslims in European History while I am here."

"Here is a map of the Ottoman Empire right here," said Tony pointing to a map on the wall at the end of the hallway.

"I didn't realize!" said Hannah, genuinely surprised.

"Understandable," said Tony. "You've studied American history. Isn't that right? All two hundred years of it!"

Just then Mrs. Boyce walked up to Hannah and Tony.

"Hannah dear, how was the Calistoga party? I'm sorry that you girls missed it. Did they have fun? Was Gerry there?" Mrs. Boyce asked with a twinkle.

"Before you go, can you take a picture with me, Mrs. Boyce? Your Chardonnay is known throughout the world," said Tony stepping next to Mrs. Boyce.

"Certainly, Tony." The event photographer snapped their picture.

"Come; let's see the magnificent art treasures in this building."

"Grandma, Tony said that he is related to the Vasari that painted these walls. Is that possible?"

"Well, the Persians did have a delegation in Genoa in the 1500s, close to here. It is possible."

"What? Tony is related to Vasari?" said Eduardo as he and Niki joined them at the wine-tasting station. "That is the best one yet. I wonder why he is so determined to become an Italian."

"Well, Grandma, I believe we can legally drink here," said Hannah. "What do you say Niki? How about if I tell you which Chardonnay is the best here?" Hannah teased.

"That's hilarious," said Mrs. Boyce, not taking the bait.

"Okay," said Hannah. "Back to the sparkling cider. I wish they had a Coke at least."

"Let me share some of the fantastic stories about this place," Eduardo said, taking Hannah's hand and leading them to an enormous curving staircase. Hannah was thrilled that Eduardo took her hand and smiled gleefully over her shoulder at Niki.

"Palazzo Vecchio was built over fifteen years, starting in 1299," said Eduardo. "It almost looks like a fort, but inside we have fabulous treasures by the best Italian artists that ever lived. The Medici family paid the best artists to decorate this palace, and we are restoring the works room by room."

"What is the lion climbing up the pole at the top of the building?" asked Hannah.

"That lion is a symbol of Florence," replied Eduardo. "He shows our leadership, our prowess, our pride in our accomplishments. The clock below it has worked perfectly since the fourteenth century, when the government of Florence moved here. The government is still here on the second floor. Back then, the workers had to stay here night and day for two months at a time."

"How come?" asked Hannah.

"Florentines wanted to make sure that their civil servants were not distracted by business or personal matters when they were here," said Eduardo. "That way they tended only to government matters. The comfort and security of the city's residents were assured by the workers being here on site. The Italian wine consortium has offices down here around the corner."

"This room rocks!" said Niki as they stepped down into a huge room with gigantic paintings on every wall.

"This is the *Salone Del Cinquecento*," said Mrs. Boyce. "The ceiling is covered with gilded wood ornaments and is painted with scenes of the history of Florence."

"Wow. You guys have been in battles for centuries," said Niki.

"Yes, unfortunately, war has been with us since Cain and Abel," said Eduardo. "We Florentines have to defend this beautiful place from others who want it. You Americans have been lucky. Only Japan has attacked you on your soil."

"Yes," said Mrs. Boyce, "And we chased them all over the Pacific Ocean and then bombed them on their own soil for that! No punishment would have been enough! My uncle and many of his friends were killed at Pearl Harbor. My mother was never the same after that. To just attack us, murder us, without a declaration of war! It was criminal!"

"Are any of these by Michelangelo?" asked Hannah, setting up her miniature digital camera and trying to stop her grandmother's passionate views on the bombing of Pearl Harbor. She looked around to see if there were any Japanese tourists around. Luckily, she could not see any in the immediate vicinity. The worst time was when she visited Pearl Harbor. Grandma could not understand why the Japanese were allowed to visit the *USS Arizona* monument when they were the ones who had ambushed the United States there. It was totally embarrassing. Hannah did not understand why Grandma would not get over it and move on.

"Actually, these were all originally frescoed by Michelangelo and Leonardo da Vinci. Michelangelo was supposed to paint the *Battle of Cascina*, but he didn't finish it and da Vinci tried a new paint technique that didn't work. So neither project was finished. All the paintings here are by Giorgio Vasari."

"Oh!" said Niki. "Tony's ancestors. I never knew that the Persians were in Genoa."

"I will have to look into that," said Eduardo. "This is the first time I've heard that Tony is related to Vasari."

"Let's go up to the wardrobe room," said Mrs. Boyce. "When the Medici family moved in here in 1540, they redecorated. The wardrobe room is not a clothes closet. It is filled with paintings of voyages and adventures. It is my favorite."

"Wow," said Hannah, entering the wardrobe room. "Look at the armoires with the old maps on them!"

"These maps represent the way the world was in the sixteenth century," said Eduardo.

"Cool," said Niki. "Wow! Here is Persia! Look how much land they had! Boy, the world has changed since then. I wonder how it will change after we are dead?"

"Pleasant," replied Hannah. "Us dying is a long way off, hopefully. Look at this globe! It is huge!"

The four wandered from room to spectacular room, each room revealing a new dimension to the complicated and amazing Italian history.

"If you want to see something by Michelangelo, let's go outside," said Eduardo when they had completed the tour.

As they descended the main staircase, Eduardo pointed to a rock up to the right of the door.

"What is that?" asked Niki.

"The rumor is that Michelangelo, to win a bet, sculpted it with his back turned, so he could not see what he was doing!" said Eduardo.

Hannah whipped out her camera. "Now this rocks! Okay, time to eat!"

They all laughed and walked across the plaza to the apartment door.

"You're right," said Grandma. "Jet lag is starting to kick in. Let's go in and get something to eat and get to bed early. Eduardo, thank you so much for escorting us to the wine show. It was delightful."

As Eduardo left, both girls hung out the door and watched him walk down the steps.

"He's *so* Italian," Niki cooed.

"Way cool," Hannah added, shoving Niki aside so she could get a better last look at him.

A few minutes after he left, as Mrs. Boyce was preparing a quick snack for them to eat before bed, the door buzzer sounded.

Buzz Buzz!

"I wonder who that could be," Mrs. Boyce asked herself as she walked to the intercom. "Who is it?" She spoke clearly into the intercom.

"It's me, *Signora*. Tony Vasari." Tony's voice sounded smooth and in complete control.

"What can I do for you, Tony? It's late, and we're very tired up here."

"I'm sorry to bother you so late. But *Signorina* Jordan left her computer in my office, and I wanted to get it back to her."

"Please come up." Mrs. Boyce pressed the button that opens the exterior door.

"I can't believe I forgot it," Hannah said, bolting toward the door and down the steps.

"Thank you so much, Mr. Vasari," Hannah said as she took the computer case from him.

"I'm so glad you brought this back to me," Hannah sighed. "I'm sure I would have missed it in a minute or two, and I would have been very upset if it got locked up in your office overnight."

"I knew you would want your computer, so I brought it over as soon as I saw it sitting there," he grinned.

"Thank you very much, Tony," Mrs. Boyce added, hoping he would just leave without having to be invited in. "The young ladies are getting ready to retire. Please excuse us," she added, hoping once again he would just leave.

Standing there, as if oblivious to Mrs. Boyce, Tony started rambling on about how he had been the center of attention at the winery party and how he hoped that Mrs. Boyce had been able to acquire the root stock she had hoped to purchase.

Pointing Tony toward the door, Mrs. Boyce's voice became firm. "We will see you tomorrow," she said as she closed the door behind him.

"I thought he would never leave," she sighed as she turned her attention back to her two young charges. "Let's have something to eat and get a good night's rest. We have a lot to do tomorrow."

"Thanks, Grandma. That Tony was nice to bring my laptop back, but he sure acted like he'd like to hang around us just a bit too much."

"He gives me the creeps," Niki said shrugging her shoulders.

Suddenly, Hannah, Niki, and Mrs. Boyce started yawning. They all got jet lag at the same time.

"I love this pasta," Hannah grinned at her grandmother as she loaded on some butter and stuffed the pasta into her mouth.

"Me, too," Niki said, shoveling in a huge bite herself.

They chatted and helped Grandma wash the dishes before they all crashed into bed.

Later that night, Hannah woke up to loud slamming noises. "Grandma?" she called out. She quickly realized that no one was awake but her. Hannah slipped out of bed and cautiously unclipped the mini-flashlight that was hooked onto her backpack. All of the windows and shutters were open and smashing against the building wildly.

"How did these get open?" she wondered, struggling to close the heavy wooden windows in her and Niki's room. She went from room to room, closing the shutters and windows. "Why didn't anyone else hear these shutters?" she wondered, a little annoyed that she had to close all these windows by herself in the dark.

Finally, she pulled the last shutter in with all her might and went back to bed. She felt uneasy, but she didn't know why. Suddenly she remembered Tony's story about the spirits foretelling tragedy with the flapping windows, and she shivered. After staring at the ceiling for what seemed like hours, she fell into a fitful sleep. Little did she know that the spirits were telling her that something terrible was about to happen.

Chapter 4
Touring Florence

*N*iki woke up with shopping on her mind. Her mother had given her a list and her Visa card. Niki was pleased that her mother trusted her not only with picking out the right things but with the credit card, too. Niki's mother told her to "be thrifty," but she was allowed to buy herself and Hannah "something gold and special" to remember Florence.

Niki wasn't much on fancy clothes, preferring to be a lot less conspicuous than her movie-star mother. However, Niki's sense of good taste was well developed from fifteen years of living with her artist father as well as her flamboyant mother.

This morning, Niki picked up her journal and made a few entries before Hannah and Mrs. Boyce were awake.

Dear Diary,

Today is fantabulous already. The vendor-cart man was up early with his dappled gray horse. I saw him stop and feed his horse an apple in the middle of the plaza just before dawn. What a beautiful sight. I was sitting at this window when the sun came up this morning. The pink clouds drifted softly on the pale blue sky as the golden rays of the sun warmed the cobblestones in the Piazza Della Signoria. Yikes, Diary, I'm starting to sound like my father the artist! I guess it could be worse.

Today I'm going to get some shopping in. We've been here over a day already, and I haven't been in one shop. This will be the day I shop till I drop!

Got to run. The gang is coming alive, and I want to get the first shower before the hot water runs out.

Hugs for today,

N

With that brief sign-off, Niki grabbed her towel and her robe and literally ran to the shower room just as Hannah and Mrs. Boyce were entering the kitchen.

"I'm first today," Niki gleefully grinned as she closed the sliding door to the tiny room.

"Make it snappy, beauty queen," Hannah retorted. "There are some real women out here, and we need hot water, too."

Niki pretended to not hear Hannah's plea and turned the hot water to maximum. Working quickly with her favorite shampoo and cream rinse, Niki sang her favorite little tune as she rinsed her hair to squeaky clean.

Hannah could hear Niki sing "Zippity Doo Dah" in the shower. "Hey, you, movie queen. You're singing *my* song," Hannah yelled as she teasingly pounded on the bathroom door.

Niki yelled back, "You didn't write it, did you, dork?" Not wanting to hang anyone up, Niki finished the shower, pulled her robe around her, and darted out of the bathroom.

Niki poked Hannah in the shoulder, and dashed by her to their bedroom.

"I'll be ready in one minute. Don't dork around, dorkette, or this bus is leavin' without yah."

"Now, Niki," Mrs. Boyce interjected. "You aren't going anywhere without a proper breakfast."

Niki smiled at Mrs. Boyce and said softly, "I'll make you breakfast, eat breakfast, wash the dishes, and plant a garden, and Hannah will still be in there messing with her hair. She has no idea just how beautiful she is. Those aristocratic cheekbones and that beautiful hair with those natural highlights—to die for—but she's very slow in the morning."

Mrs. Boyce laughed and nodded. "You're right about that. Hannah can get caught up in her thoughts and lose track of time. I'll nudge her along a bit. You go get yourself ready. You talk a fast streak, but if you'll notice, I am the only one actually ready to begin the day."

Niki blushed. "Oh, no, I'm outta here," she joked. Niki made the roadrunner maneuver with her elbows in the air and dashed out of the kitchen into her room as Mrs. Boyce laughed merrily.

"Niki loosens Hannah up, which is great," thought Mrs. Boyce. "Such a nice person and smart too, just like Hannah." Ever since the girls teamed up to solve the *Witness in Wine Country* mystery, Mrs. Boyce appreciated what a great team they were. Hannah was a kindhearted, smart, and talented girl and a blossoming beauty in the Anglo/Irish tradition. Hannah was already dealing with a nasty divorce. Niki was the smart and funny daughter of a movie star. Her parents were still happily married. Niki's beauty was already apparent, but Niki was determined to hide it, knowing the fake attention it could bring. "They are a good combination," reflected Mrs. Boyce contentedly.

Finally, both girls were completely dressed and sitting at the table in the kitchen gobbling down their breakfasts of scrambled eggs and bacon. Actually, Hannah ate only bacon and toast. Eggs weren't her favorite food. But bacon was, and her grandmother always made sure there was plenty on hand no matter where they were. Mrs. Boyce truly adored her granddaughter and without reservation spoiled her as much as was possible.

Breakfast finished, both girls headed for their toothbrushes. Without even discussing it, Hannah headed toward the shower room, and Niki headed toward the powder room, both rooms having sinks, so they could get their dental hygiene accomplished at the same time. After so many years of being best friends, Niki and Hannah seemed to zing along on the same wavelength. They said that they could read each other's mind.

"Let's go shop for the gold my mom said we could get!" exclaimed Niki happily. "I'm thinking about matching bracelets or watches; that way we can always remember this fun trip. I'm finally acclimated and ready to explore! Let's go right now!"

"Me, too," agreed Hannah. "But aren't we on vacation? Can we turn down the Niki speed to about 40 miles per hour instead of the current 60 MPH?" Hannah scrambled to get her spare hair-tie, her wallet, brush, and shopping list for friends back home into her day-pack.

"You're right. You are the only person who could say that to me, you know that?" said Niki fondly.

"Bye, girls! I'm off to the wine show again," said Mrs. Boyce with a smile. "Today I will convince Mr. Felini to sell me some vines for that Chardonnay I admired yesterday. I will meet you back here in two hours."

Just before they stepped out of the apartment door, Niki looked Hannah over. Smiling, she patted her friend on the back and said, "You look great today, Hannah. Your outfit matches perfectly—blouse, shorts, socks, and shoes. Very coordinated. Tell the truth. Did your grandmother pick that outfit out for you?"

"Of course. I will never have the natural outfits savvy, so I need help and admit it. My mother may not be a movie star, but Grandma takes care of me. Don't you, Grandma? Thanks, Grandma, for mixing comfort with style. At least that's what it said on the tag I just removed," Hannah said with a laugh, giving her grandmother a hug.

"Last person down the stairs gets the bathroom last for the rest of the trip," Hannah barbed as they bolted down the steps two at a time, glad to be on their own in one of the coolest towns in Europe.

"Keep up, dorkette, and be careful on these winding stairs. I don't want to have to call a cute Italian doctor to fix you up if you fall down the steps," said Hannah. Niki raced after her, but Hannah was down first.

Once out the door, it was only about three steps around the corner and into the main part of the plaza. The sun was shining brightly as they strolled into the Piazza Della Signoria. Several tour guides, lofting signs on sticks and flags to help the tourists follow them around, were beginning to gather their troops. In addition to the Palazzo Vecchio and the famous Uffizi Gallery, mostly five-hundred-year-old, two-story brick buildings surrounded the Piazza Della Signoria.

"I wish I could have met Michelangelo when he was nineteen and bursting with hope and talent. I bet he was a hunk," said Niki wistfully as she looked up at *Neptune's Fountain.*

"Now, that would be a romance," agreed Hannah. "I would like to have fallen in love with da Vinci— handsome and used both sides of his brain at the genius level! I can just feel all that talent packed into this plaza, and it's five hundred years later!"

"Where to first, Yogi?" Hannah asked Niki. Niki was turning a street map over and over in her hands.

"Man, this map is impossible," Niki exclaimed, crumpling it up in a ball and tossing it into the one trash can they could find on the plaza. "Speaking of geniuses, a lot of them are buried at the church on Santa Croce Plaza. Let's make sure to get over there. Oh! And Galileo's middle finger is on display at the Science Museum. Let's go over there first," she said mischievously.

"No problem for me," replied Hannah. "Today I will follow you, and tomorrow you can do what I want to do. I've got the address of our apartment written on this piece of paper," Hannah said, pulling a slip of paper rubber-banded around Hannah's copy of the apartment key. "I'm all set," she said as she stuffed the wad back into her pocket.

"Great, let's go this way." Niki motioned to the left and began to walk. "Sure is bright out here. I wish I had remembered to bring my sunglasses from home. Who knew it was going to feel like summer here in the middle of September?" Niki remarked, squinting and putting her hand over her eyes to shield them from the sun's glare.

"Too bad, Niki," Hannah grinned as she pulled her sunglasses out of her pocket and plopped them on her nose. "I remembered." Hannah thought, "Really, Grandma remembered, but Niki doesn't need to know that." They were best friends with a little undercurrent of friendly competition.

The two girls made a quick loop around the plaza peeking in the brick shops and restaurants before heading out to look for the shops that Niki's mother had noted to be worthy of investigation.

"These shops probably look the same today as they did five hundred years ago," remarked Hannah with awe. "I wonder what was happening in the United States in the 1500s. Only the Native Americans were there then. Christopher Columbus only arrived in 1492. Meanwhile, over here, they were sculpting *David* and this *Fontana de Neptune, Neptune's Fountain.*"

Niki thought she noticed someone looking at her and then ducking behind the copy of the statue of *David*.

"Hannah," Niki whispered and poked Hannah with her elbow. "Someone's watching us."

"What?" Hannah yelped as if being stabbed. "Who? Where? Is it one of your mother's fans?"

"Shhh—over there," replied Niki slightly annoyed.

"Shhh yourself; over where? I don't see anyone," Hannah replied looking around. "Over there is not a specific direction."

"Don't look," repeated Niki. "Behind the *David* statue. I think it might be Tony, that guy from the winery show. Let's just ignore him and see if he follows us to the shops. Let's go." Niki grabbed Hannah's arm and began to walk quickly toward the south end of the plaza, toward the main shopping street. They didn't turn to look behind them until they had gone all the way down the alley that connects the Piazza Della Signoria and the Piazza Republica. They ducked into a doorway and peeked out.

Just then, Tony sauntered down the narrow alley in his black leather pants, looking around as if trying to find someone.

"Shhh—it's him," Niki whispered, nudging Hannah again.

"Shhh yourself. Let's just ask him. Tony?" Hannah jabbed Niki in the ribs with her elbow. "Stop jabbing me, you bully." Tony did not hear her.

"I'm sorry," Niki apologized. "It's just one of those bad habits I picked up at school. I'm not sure what Tony is up to, but now that we know he's following us, let's give him something to think about."

"Like what?" Hannah asked

"I'm not sure." Niki grabbed the clip out of her hair and tossed her head defiantly. Her blond hair cascaded around her shoulders and fell in feathery waves down her back. "There you are, Tony. Follow me." Niki squared her shoulders and stepped out onto Via Calimala, the best shopping street in the city of Florence.

Retrieving her mother's list from her pocket, Niki announced, "Gloves. Mom wants me to pick her up a pair of zebra-striped gloves at the shop called "Vesta." It's on this street somewhere."

"Zebra-striped gloves. Whatever happened to black or tan? Is it for a movie opening? Your mom is so out there, Niki," Hannah giggled.

Linking arms, they began their walk along the Via Calimala. About an hour later, the zebra-striped leather gloves safely tucked into Niki's expandable shopping bag, Niki pulled out the list again.

"Tony is two stores behind us," said Niki. "I can see him in the store window glass."

"Check. That's one off the list. Now on to the Duomo. It's the largest church in Florence. Mom wants me to look for a book in the Academia del'Opera del Duomo bookstore. She wants *Brunelleschi's Dome: How a Renaissance Genius Reinvented Architecture,* by Ross King. She could probably get this one off of Amazon.com, but she thought it would be a good exercise for me to look for it. And she said that the top of the Duomo has the best view, if you can make it to the top, that is!"

"The top of the what?" Hannah asked with alarm. "The last time you had me climbing something, it was up 325 steps to the top of the Bunker Hill monument."

"Strap on your parachute, Hannah. The tour book says it is 464 steps to the top but really worth it. It should be fun. Tag, you're it," Niki said, scooting past Hannah and heading down the street at a full run. Running was not very easy this time of day since the streets of Florence were very crowded, and Niki nearly tripped over a street vendor selling beautiful little paintings of the Duomo. When she finally came to a stop in front of the Duomo entrance, Hannah was nowhere to be seen. "Oops," Niki thought, "I didn't mean to lose Hannah in the crowd. I'll catch up with her at the top."

"Niki, we are in trouble now," Hannah thought to herself as she reached the beautiful church with the huge dome rising high above the city. "Grandma is going to never let us go out alone if we can't even stay together." Just then Hannah saw Tony standing by a newsstand pretending to read a newspaper. "There he is again. I wonder what gives with him?"

"Niki, Niki," Hannah halfheartedly called out toward the crowd. Just then Tony started walking toward her. Suddenly feeling panicked, Hannah grabbed some change out of her pocket, quickly bought a ticket for the Duomo, and dashed through the entrance gate, not checking behind her to see if Tony was following.

Hannah headed straight to the staircase and started climbing. At first, she counted the steps, but, after the second time she stopped to rest, she lost count somewhere around 165 or so. Putting her head down and breathing deeply and rhythmically like she learned in yoga class, Hannah returned to the task of climbing the stairs.

The first few sets of staircases were tight spirals with no handrails. The climb was steep, and the staircases were small and cramped. Hannah tried to imagine what it was like four hundred years ago when the cupola was being built. "It must have been very hard work to carry all the building materials up these tiny stairs," she thought.

At about what seemed to be halfway up, Hannah heard a familiar voice just above.

"Hannah, Hannah. It's me, Niki. I'm so sorry I lost you in the crowd. I got carried away, and before I knew it I'd lost you. I'm so, so sorry. I scared myself half to death."

"That's okay, Niki. I can't believe you ditched me back there. Did you see Tony?" Hannah asked.

"I thought I did see him over by the altar." said Niki. "But I haven't seen him on the stairs."

They slowly climbed the remaining stairs until they suddenly stepped out onto the skinny viewing balcony inside the bottom of the massive frescoed ceiling of the Duomo.

"Oh!" said Hannah, looking down into the church many stories below.

They both stopped in their tracks and then walked around and around the circular viewing platform, transfixed by the powerful images. Hannah looked at the guidebook.

"This is *The Last Judgment*," said Hannah, pointing up to the pictures. "See? Some people are going to heaven, and those other poor slobs are going to hell. Ick! That one guy is being eaten!"

"I didn't know that there were any frescos with pictures like this," Hannah said.

"Wow, these are the weirdest things I've ever seen," Niki remarked.

"Hello, girls," said Tony, suddenly appearing on the viewing platform high above the church floor.

"Hi, Tony," said Hannah warily. "I thought I saw you outside the church."

"Ladies, look over here at this three-headed dragon. In the *Book of Revelations* in the *Bible*, the Beast from the Sea had many heads, and it was feared because it could fight a holy war and conquer the enemies of God. We Muslims believe that, too. Books from the Old Testament, as you call it, are used by many different religions."

"Pretty scary symbolism for the inside of a church," said Niki.

"You got that right," Hannah agreed. "I can see where people back then were scared straight if this is what they thought hell was like!"

"It is good to fight in a holy war," said Tony. "Where I come from, we call it a *jihad*. Those fighting in it go to heaven. You Christians fought holy wars called Crusades."

"Well, Tony, that was a long time ago. If you'll excuse us, we've got to go up to the top. We have to meet my grandmother soon," said Hannah.

"*Ciao*," said Tony as he turned to go back down the stairs.

"Yes, let's keep going and get to the top," Niki urged Hannah, moving to the doorway leading to the next set of stairs and pushing Hannah through it.

"Nice history lesson," said Hannah collapsing with laughter on the stairs.

The last leg of the climb had very small steps that climbed up the inside seam of the dome itself.

"This feels like a rounded cave," said Hannah, touching the ceiling. "This roof is about an inch above our heads! Claustrophobia to the max!"

Finally, they stuck their heads out of the stairwell into the open air. The view was simply spectacular. The girls climbed carefully onto the marble platform and looked around.

"Oh, no!" said Niki as she slipped on the wet marble and her legs dangled dangerously off the ledge.

"Oh, my God," shouted Hannah, grabbing Niki's hand and pulling her away from the edge clumsily.

Niki jumped up like nothing happened, brushed herself off, and pulled out her camera in one motion.

"Hannah, stand over by the rail. I want to take your picture." Niki motioned toward the side of the platform.

"Is this a good pose?" Hannah mugged a goofy smile and crossed her eyes.

"Great," quipped Niki as she snapped the picture. "Wow! The view is super! You can see the whole city from here! Can you find our apartment building?"

"Sure. It's over there by the Palazzo Vecchio. I can see the roof and part of the alley next to the building," Hannah remarked, pulling her opera glasses out of her pocket. As she unwound the neck strap from around the glasses, she heard a faint tinkling clank sound from beneath her feet.

"Oh, great, I wonder what that was?" Hannah thought, looking at her feet but not seeing anything.

Before Hannah could think about it any longer, Niki grabbed her arm and dragged her to the other side of the platform. "Look over there." Niki pointed in the direction of hills next to the town. "Does that look like something is on fire?"

"No. It just looks like some fireplace smoke to me," Hannah answered.

Just then a man stepped out from the stairway and grabbed something off the platform where the girls were previously standing, bolted by the girls, and headed down the narrow entrance to the return stairwell.

"Was that Tony?" Niki asked Hannah.

"I don't know. I didn't see who it was very clearly," Hannah answered. "What the heck is up with that guy? He was such a kiss-up at the party. I guess if Grandma isn't with us, we just don't count. For a good-looking guy, he is mysterious. And what was up with that *jihad* stuff?"

"Let's get going. I'm starting to get a nosebleed from this altitude," Niki joked and ushered Hannah to the entrance to the stairwell. "Be careful now, Hannah. I don't want to have to bring you back to the apartment in a cast."

"Don't worry about me, Little Miss Clumsy Locks. I can take care of myself. You watch out for yourself."

The trip down the stairs went a lot quicker than the trip up, but it was still a very scary descent. On the way down, they couldn't help but look down, and it always seemed like the tunnel was too narrow to get through.

"We'd better hurry," Hannah said, looking at her watch as they reached the bottom. "We promised Grandma we'd meet her at noon. We have tickets to see the real statue of David, and we still haven't found that book for your mother."

"Let's just head out and find that book right now," Niki said as she dashed through the exit door and turned right toward the Duomo museum and bookstore.

Inside the Opera Della Duomo Museum, they found that they had to go all the way through the museum to get to the bookstore. As they walked through the various rooms, they encountered one of the most beautiful statues they'd ever seen, Michelangelo's *Pieta*. The largest figure, the one holding the figure of Christ, was supposed to have been carved by Michelangelo as a self-portrait. Both girls just stood there in awe of this magnificent work of art.

"It's so strong and passionate, and it was just a big hunk of rock," Niki commented.

"That is so cool that Michelangelo put himself in the sculpture," replied Hannah. "I wish I could see him when he was younger than that. It says here that he really didn't believe in God until he was in his seventies! Unbelievable that he painted and sculpted all those statues of Jesus, Mary, and creation, before he believed it himself!"

Once in the bookstore, they quickly located the book for Niki's mother, paid for it with her credit card, and headed in a rush to the Galleria dell' Academia to meet Mrs. Boyce.

"Hi, girls," Mrs. Boyce greeted Hannah and Niki with a big hug. "Have you had a nice morning?" Mrs. Boyce looked simply stunning in her sunny yellow jacket over a white blouse and perfectly pressed khaki trousers. Her hair, pulled up into a knot, was held in place by a matching yellow chiffon scarf.

"We had a great time, Grandma," said Hannah. "We climbed to the top of the Duomo and had a look around. It was fabulous."

"Well, I'm glad you made it back here in time. I've been reading about that diamond robbery you girls heard about on the Internet while on the plane, and it seems that security here in Florence is going to be tightened quite a lot. We may be searched before we go in this museum, so I'm glad you made it with a little extra time."

As it turned out, no one was searching anyone at the Galleria dell' Academia. The line to get into the museum wound completely around the block and onto the next. Just getting in without a reservation required a wait of about four hours. Hannah, Niki, and Mrs. Boyce walked right in at their appointed time using the tickets that Hannah had bought on the Internet.

"The Internet! Gotta love it," Hannah quipped as they passed the hundreds of people in line.

Once inside the museum, they were surprised to see that there were only four rooms in the Academia. The Academia houses probably the most beautiful statue ever carved, "The David," as the people of Florence refer to the statue.

Mrs. Boyce took her time looking at the eight slave statues that lined the room in front of the great statue, but Hannah and Niki made a beeline right to the foot of the pedestal and gazed at the enormous marble statue.

"This is the most beautiful statue I have ever seen. It almost looks like he's breathing, even without clothes on," Hannah said with a big smile to Niki behind Mrs. Boyce's back.

"The people of Florence say it captures David's face after he killed Goliath, but Michelangelo said he sculpted David before David killed Goliath. "What do you girls think?" asked Mrs. Boyce as she joined the girls at the statue.

"The expression on his face is so real," Niki said. "I think it could be after—he is stunned that he killed that huge giant with a sling shot against all odds! Let's go near his face," said Niki, dragging Hannah over to the other side of the statue.

"Hannah, is that Tony over there?" Niki poked Hannah in the side and motioned toward a man over near Mrs. Boyce. "What is he doing? It looks like he's looking in your grandmother's shopping bag. I don't like it."

"I'm only going to say this one more time. Stop poking me," Hannah said sternly to Niki.

"Oh, rats, I keep forgetting you are a tender little flower," Niki joked.

"Bite me, brat!" Hannah said with an equally as snotty grin.

"Look at what he's doing now, Hannah. He's putting something into your grandma's bag. I'm going to get to the bottom of what he's up to." Niki headed toward Mrs. Boyce.

"Tony. Hey, Tony. It's us, Niki and Hannah. What are you doing?" Niki shouted as loudly as seemed appropriate in a solemn museum.

Tony, seeing Niki and Hannah approach, turned on his heels, ran out the front door of the museum, and ducked down an alley before the girls could get through the crowd and out the door.

"That was weird," Hannah thought. "Grandma, we thought we saw a man drop something into your bag. Is there anything strange in there?"

Mrs. Boyce looked into her bag, and right there was a piece of paper with the apartment number and street address on it wrapped around a key.

"Hannah, that looks like your key!" said Niki alarmed.

Hannah searched frantically into her pockets and found that her key was missing. "Oh, my God! How did he get my key?" asked Hannah. "Should we call the police?"

"Girls, hold on. We have no proof that he did anything," said Mrs. Boyce.

"Why is he everywhere we go?" asked Niki. "I don't like it. It's like those paparazzi that follow my mother! What could we possibly have that a rich descendant of Vasari would want?"

"What about fingerprints?" asked Hannah.

"Oh, do you have a kit with you?" joked Niki.

"And we have little probable cause," agreed Mrs. Boyce. "But he bears watching, good looking or not. I am in awe of this statue. It is the embodiment of true talent and art. Now, let's go get some lunch."

"Sounds good to me!" Hannah and Niki said in unison.

Chapter 5
Tragedy in the USA!

"I'm telling you, Mrs. Boyce, the best restaurant in Florence is on the river. You and the girls would love it!" raved the retired pilot at lunch at the café right on Signoria Piazza. The tiny inside of the restaurant had only one table, and the heavyset owner sat as lord of his red-and-white checkered tablecloth fiefdom on the plaza. Mrs. Boyce, Hannah, and Niki ate outside in the fresh air.

"Aren't you sick of this pizza by now? I've seen you and the girls ordering the Marguerite pizza for lunch and dinner for two days now. There *is* good food in Florence!"

"Well now, Josh, we haven't had it everyday," said Mrs. Boyce. "But you are right. I do prefer the American Italian food: veal Parmesan, spring pasta, and fresh crisp romaine lettuce. In California, we are very spoiled with fresh vegetables and fresh pasta."

"Grandma, maybe he's right," interjected Hannah. "I mean, I like tomato-and-cheese pizza, but it costs a fortune in this place. And they burned the crust last night and now again at lunch. Maybe we should try to eat out again. I know I was whining about the food and my upset stomach, but I'll try again if you and Niki will."

"I'm not ready. I'm sorry, but they don't seem to be able to spell refrigeration over here," said Niki.

"What kind of food do they have, Mr. Roth?" Hannah asked, not able to resist another shot at something delicious.

"They have fresh shrimp scampi, steak, hamburgers, French fries, and northern Italian dishes, too. I took my seventeen-year-old there last winter. You have to walk over the Ponte Vecchio to get to it, though. They don't take phone reservations. Or are you teens allergic to walking?" he said with a wry smile.

"Hamburgers! Real hamburgers? And French fries, not wet greasy potatoes?" asked Hannah excitedly.

"Real hamburgers," said the pilot. "I would not lie to a teen about that!"

"Honestly, Hannah, we have not been away *that* long. I realize that we are in a holding pattern here at the café, but I see your cheeseburger craving is rearing up," said Mrs. Boyce.

"Hey, mine, too! I'm up for a hamburger, if you can get a tasty meal, too, Mrs. Boyce," said Niki, suddenly more interested.

"All right, let's pay the check, make a little visit to the apartment, and head over there," said Mrs. Boyce.

The girls laughed. Mrs. Boyce prided herself on the fact that they had not had to use a public restroom since they got to Florence. Florence does not provide public toilets, so tourists and residents alike have to beg at restaurants to use theirs, which are often filthy. The girls discovered that on the way back from the Duomo. Luckily their apartment on Signoria Piazza was the perfect location to walk to anything. They had not been in a car since they arrived.

"Girls, let me give you the tour," said Mrs. Boyce, walking quickly up to the bridge.

"All these stores used to be butcheries until the fifteenth century when a grand duke kicked out the butchers and replaced them with high quality goldsmiths. He gave each goldsmith a house with a storefront, a work area in back, and a residence upstairs. Many of the same families still own these places!"

"This is the only bridge on the Arno River not bombed by Hitler in World War II. The Nazis were occupying Italy and decided to burn down the bridges over the Arno River to slow down the Allies so that they would not catch them as they retreated. They burned each bridge, but when they got to the Ponte Vecchio they decided to destroy the houses at each end of the bridge and left the bridge alone.

"No cars are allowed on the bridge anymore, but wall-to-wall tourists pack the cobblestone streets jostling for the precious wares," finished Mrs. Boyce.

"'When in Italy, get some gold' is what my mother says," said Niki. "She gave me some money for a gold watch. I'll look on the way back from making reservations. I love this place—one beautiful trinket after the next and all unique!"

"Since many of these artisans are descendants of the original shop owners from the fifteenth century," said Mrs. Boyce, "this gold jewelry is the most interesting and beautiful I've seen so far in the world."

"Now that is saying something, Grandma!" laughed Hannah, knowing her grandmother's jewelry expertise.

"Look here, girls. This is the bust of Benvenuto Cellini, one of the greatest goldsmiths that Florence has ever seen," said Mrs. Boyce. The trio could not help pausing to look in the shops. At midspan of the Ponte Vecchio, Hannah and Niki stopped for a picture. Little did they know, it would be the last smiling picture in Florence that they took.

"I think it is down this way," said Niki, looking at the street map. "It is supposed to be on the river. Let's just keep walking down the street. I don't see a porch on the river. It's called 'Pasquale's.' Do you see a sign?"

"There! There it is!" said Hannah. They raced over to the restaurant and found a menu mounted on the outside door.

Quickly scanning it, Hannah said, "It's true! It's true! Cheeseburgers—scampi, too, Grandma! Let's find the manager so we can make a reservation!"

Hannah knocked on the door vigorously.

The chef hesitantly came to the door. Obviously it was not open yet.

"Can we make reservations?" asked Hannah.

"*Bon giorno,*" said the chef as he unlocked the door. He proffered the reservations book. "You sure you want to eat here tonight? With all that has happened?" he asked with a thick accent.

Thinking that he was talking about the diamond robberies, Hannah said, "Sure, dinner for three! Can we sit on the porch?" She continued pointing to it just in case the chef did not quite understand English. The quaint porch hung out over the river.

Niki walked over. "This is beautiful! I can see why that pilot liked it. This is going to be great!"

"Okay, girls, I agree. This will do just fine. I'm looking forward to it," agreed Mrs. Boyce as they left the restaurant.

"Are you Americans? Are you Americans?" cried a sobbing woman running up to them.

Mrs. Boyce instinctively moved in front of the teens, and they in turn slid to each side of Mrs. Boyce to protect her. "Yes, we're Americans. You sound American, too," said Mrs. Boyce, "Why do you ask?"

"I am American! I am American! We've been attacked!" sobbed the woman.

"Terrorists have attacked us! They attacked the World Trade Center in New York!" continued the woman hysterically. "Haven't you seen a TV? Haven't you heard? The whole world is different! It's worse than Pearl Harbor! They attacked the Pentagon, too!"

All three stared at the crying woman now to size her up. She wore a crinkly purple crepe skirt that flowed to the ground and Birkenstocks. She looked to be about forty-five or so, and she clearly had been crying. She didn't look exactly credible, but she didn't look like a street person either.

"Miss, what do you mean?" asked Mrs. Boyce. "What has happened? We have not seen a TV today."

"I'm telling you. We've been attacked!" repeated the woman.

"How? Did they put another bomb in the World Trade Center garage?" asked Hannah. Her mother taught at Columbia University in New York City and had been at a meeting in the World Trade Center during the last bombing in 1993. Hannah's mother escaped, but ever since, Hannah hated when her mother went there. She read the reports on the Internet about how hard it would be to put out a fire in that building because of the height and the sheer number of floors and offices. Hannah felt a sense of dread.

"Just a minute, Hannah, no one said a bomb. Miss, please explain yourself. We all have relatives in New York," said Mrs. Boyce.

"Forget this pathetic woman!" said Niki, whose mother had a premiere in New York and was there now with her Dad. "Where was she staying?" thought Niki. "Where was she?" "Let's get to a TV and get some facts now!" Niki suggested.

"That's not going to be easy," remarked Hannah, alarmed. "I didn't mind not having a TV in the apartment until now. Let's find a TV! We don't have a phone there either, Grandma! Our American cell phones don't work here! What are we going to do?"

Hannah turned to the woman who had her face in her hands. Hannah gently put her hands on the woman's shoulders.

"What happened? Please tell us what you know in two sentences," Hannah pleaded emphatically.

"It wasn't a bomb," stammered the woman. "They flew planes into the twin towers like missiles!" continued the woman, frantically pushing her hair back from her forehead over and over. "One into one tower and another plane into the other tower! The fire and explosion was so huge that both buildings collapsed with people inside! People were jumping to the ground from the 110th floor! They crashed a plane into the Pentagon, too! Oh, my God! I heard that they are flying a plane to San Francisco to crash one there!"

Hannah remembered her visit to the World Trade Center Windows on the World restaurant. She had lunch there last year with her mother for her birthday.

Hannah had raced through her meal to get out as soon as possible. It was just too high up for Hannah.

When she was up there, she felt like she was on the upper side of a big rectangle just sticking out of the ground. She imagined it just toppling over and a shiver ran through her. In a flash, she felt that the story could be true.

"Who did it? Where is the nearest TV that we can watch?" asked Mrs. Boyce firmly, clearly alarmed.

"There's one in the Intercontinental Hotel down the street. You can get Italian cell phones on Medici Street behind Signoria Piazza." The woman ran up to another group of tourists. "Are you American?"

"What an ass," sneered Hannah worriedly.

"Let's head back to the apartment," said Mrs. Boyce. "On the way back, we'll find out what happened, and we'll get cell phones so we can call home. Let's hold hands. Do not run ahead, and from now on, watch what you say to everyone," she continued. "We do not have any rights here, girls, and everyone can tell we're Americans. If indeed it is a terrorist attack, we could be targets as Americans. We have to be very careful. I can count on you, right, girls?"

"You know you can count on us!" said both girls, hugging Mrs. Boyce tight for just a minute.

"First, we need to find out what happened, and for that we need CNN. Let's go," said Mrs. Boyce.

"I see the Intercontinental Hotel!" said Hannah. Hannah was feeling nauseous. She was resisting believing it, but she had the feeling that it was true and really bad. Did her mother die this time? She could feel a tear slide down her face, but it seemed outside herself. What had she said to her the last time? Did she tell her that she loved her? She desperately tried to remember the conversation as they hurried up the cobblestone streets.

Oh, no, Brian! Hannah felt overwhelmed by panic.

"Grandma, Brian works on the 106th floor!" Hannah said out loud, almost by mistake.

"Maybe he wasn't at work yet, darling," said Mrs. Boyce.

They looked at each other knowingly but said nothing out loud. They both knew that Brian told anyone who would listen that "I start the day to 6:00 AM every weekday! When the overseas markets are open, I'm at my desk!"

Once inside the hotel, they rushed into the bar where they could hear the TV. The smoky place was crowded. Just as they arrived, a family got up to leave and gave them their table. The parents and both kids were crying. Niki and Hannah stared at each other with fear in their eyes and the silent acknowledgment between them that something terrible had happened.

Hannah could see tears on Niki's face. "What are you thinking about, Niki?" she asked, holding her hand.

"It's my mom. You know how she and your mother love that Windows on the World. She and Dad are in New York for the debut of the film! She could easily be up there for breakfast before the promo stuff starts for the day."

"I know," said Hannah. "My mother could be there, too. And I know Brian was probably up there. Everything seems surreal and bad all of a sudden. I almost don't want to find out what happened. We were having so much fun just a few minutes ago!"

Slowly Hannah and Niki slid into the leather seats and looked up at the TV mounted on the wall.

Aaron Brown from CNN was on TV. As they sat there, a video played of the second plane driving right into the World Trade Center and exploding, followed by video of the towers collapsing and people running for their lives.

"Oh, my God!" shrieked Niki. "I can't believe it! They killed the people on the plane and the people in the building!"

"Tragically, you're right! Is this the first time you've seen it? Can you believe this is happening?" asked a twenty-something woman with short blond hair at the next table sympathetically.

"Yes," said Mrs. Boyce. "Please tell us everything that happened."

"Those Arab bastards drove two 757s into the World Trade Center, that's what!" said a big bald guy with an Arkansas Razorbacks sweatshirt on. He looked like an ex-football player.

"It's that bin Laden that had the suicide bombers hit the *USS Cole* last year!" He continued. "If that lily-livered Clinton hadn't been busy bonking Lewinsky, maybe he could have gotten rid of him.

"If the FBI hadn't been looking into Clinton's sex life instead of bin Laden, maybe we could have prevented this! Now look what's happened! They also crashed a plane into the Pentagon!" He picked up his chair and slammed it down hard on the floor and slammed back down into the chair.

Hannah and Niki rolled their eyes and turned back to the TV.

"Like he has the inside scoop on world affairs," whispered Hannah into Niki's ear.

CNN showed the Pentagon footage. Suddenly the station switched to Italian TV, which showed people jumping from the 110-story towers to their certain deaths. Some were holding hands and would twist and turn after they jumped on the way down.

Hannah felt like she might throw up right there and worried that she might. Those poor people. They just went to work, they looked out the window, and here comes a 757 filled with people? Hannah felt sick again. "Please, God, let no one we know be dead or hurt," she prayed and then felt guilty. "I pray for everyone in the building," she corrected.

"What about San Francisco?" asked Niki. Could they have bombed her home? Niki knew she was crying, but she didn't care. She just wanted to go home.

"No, there are no plane crashes in San Francisco. Not yet anyway!" said the football player. "And of course you realize that we're all trapped here, too. Trapped in the country that rolled over for Hitler. Trapped in the country that hung Mussolini with a piano wire in a gas station! They've shut down United States air space for God-knows how long."

"What does that mean, Grandma?" asked Hannah and hugged her grandmother around her dainty waist like a six-year-old. "Are we trapped here? Can we get home?"

Niki moved her chair over closer to Mrs. Boyce. "Is he right, Mrs. Boyce?" she said, trying to keep the fear out of her voice.

"We will get home, Hannah. Don't worry," said Mrs. Boyce instantly remembering people she knew that had been stuck when a conflict with the U.S. happened and they were traveling abroad. Money, she remembered. They ditched their tickets and bought first-class tickets out.

"Do we have to leave? What is going to happen?" asked Hannah. "Grandma! Why did they do it? Are we trapped here?" she repeated, becoming aware that she was babbling but powerless to stop it for a minute.

"Because they are bastards, that's why," continued the football player. "You're damn straight we're stuck over here. Stuck on the wrong side of the border with known terrorists living in Italy. They love terrorism here. This is where the Mafia started. You've heard of them, right girls—the Sopranos?"

"Henry, you're frightening the girls. Stop shouting. It's bad enough," said his wife.

Hannah looked around the smoke-filled bar with her head down and eyes tilted up, looking through her bangs. The sweatshirts, windbreakers, and running shoes told her that most of the people in the bar were Americans. All shapes, sizes, and ages, and all were crying, including Niki, Mrs. Boyce, and herself, who were still holding hands.

"Look at this! Living color! Our fellow Americans jumping, our buildings burning, business people running for their lives from a black cloud of debris chasing them down the street in New York City, the greatest city in the world! Do you know the kind of toxic crap that is in that cloud?" roared the football player, standing up and pounding the bar table with his fists. All the drinks jumped up for a minute and then back down.

"Look at those police staggering down the street, coughing, and covered with soot! The firefighters are digging in a burning graveyard with their bare hands with fire and smoke all around them! I want to puke!"

"Thousands missing! Hundreds of firefighters missing! Emergency command center was in the towers! They got us good! I feel like taking a hike over to Afghanistan and killing that bin Laden myself," shouted another guy, who looked about thirty and was balancing a squirming two-year-old boy and trying to watch the TV.

"They used our own God damn planes as cruise missiles into our proud symbol of American free trade. Those bastards! That's what we get for letting these towel-heads into our country! This is what political correctness gets you!" ranted the angry Henry again.

"Henry, you said this with the Oklahoma bombing, too, and it turned out to be one of our own citizens. Please be quiet so we can hear what happened," pleaded his wife firmly this time.

"The United States airports are all closed. There's no word yet when they will reopen," said Aaron Brown on CNN.

"Let's get some Italian cell phones and a TV if we can find one," said Mrs. Boyce.

They reluctantly got up from the table and hurried out of the bar, causing a scramble as other people tried to take their seats.

"This is a terrible situation, girls. But we are three strong women, and we are going to get through it together. The first thing we must do is locate your mothers in New York and make sure that they are safe," said Mrs. Boyce firmly. "Let's go," she said, taking both girls' hands as they started back over the crowded Ponte Vecchio.

"Just a few minutes ago we were walking over this bridge and laughing," said Niki. "No fun window-shopping on Ponte Vecchio this time. Just like those people, it started out a great day, and now they are dead."

The three huddled together and walked closely together until they got to the cell phone store described to them by the woman in the purple skirt.

"Okay," said Mrs. Boyce, holding them back for a minute before they entered the store. "We're each getting a phone with as many minutes as we can get. Provide as little information as you can inside this store. Do not let anyone know who your mothers are under any circumstances. We must be as anonymous as possible. We need to keep our options open."

Mrs. Boyce quickly made the purchases, responding to all inquiries by the clerk with "yes" or "no." They could see her brain whirring, one detail after the next. The clerk sadly shook her head at them. "We are so sorry," she repeated over and over.

"I haven't seen that look of pity for me as an American since Pearl Harbor was bombed," said Mrs. Boyce as they left the stores with their new cell phones. "I don't like it at all."

They rushed up to the apartment; put the batteries in their phones, and each started dialing.

"I can't get through. Circuits are busy!" wailed Hannah dialing her mother's office number, and then her apartment. "Please, God, do not let my mother have been in the towers today. Let her be safe." she thought.

"My mother's is busy too," said Niki dialing her mother's cell number and then her dad's.

"When you do get through, please make sure I talk to them before you hang up," replied Mrs. Boyce.

Hannah booted up her laptop and logged onto CNN.com. The same pictures from TV repeated over and over. The fire in the first tower. The plane disappearing into the second tower and exploding into a huge fireball. Sickening. She checked her mailbox, but there was no email for her.

"Check my mailbox, too," said Niki; they knew each other's passwords, so Hannah tried Niki's account. No new email there, either.

Finally Hannah reached her father on the phone. "Dad! Dad! What happened? Is everyone okay? How are Mom, Jimmy, and Brian in New York? You heard from Jimmy? Good. Good," said Hannah. "What about Brian? Was he at work? Oh. No one has heard from him?" Hannah wiped away a tear.

"Mom was in the towers? What? Are you sure that she is okay? Really? How can I get in touch with her? Tell her to send me an email right now. I hate that city. I'm glad that I live in Santa Cruz with you. I wish she had moved with us."

Niki waved her hands wildly at Hannah to signal her not to go there again with her dad. Hannah signaled back "Okay." The counselor told her a million times to let the divorce go and stop torturing he father about it. He didn't even want the divorce. "Stop it," said Hannah to herself, feeling guilty.

"No, Dad, we're okay. I don't know when we're coming back. We're not scheduled to leave until Saturday. I know. Air space is closed. I know, Dad. You're scaring me. I'll keep you posted. Here is Grandma. Bye. Love you."

"Hi, Jim," said Mrs. Boyce. "Yes, we are okay. It's terrible, I know, Jim. We will monitor the airport situation on this end, and you do it on that end; let's keep in touch by email. Thank the Lord for Hannah's laptop; we will be able to keep in touch that way. I'm sure my daughter did not realize that suicide bombers would attack the towers, or she wouldn't have gone there for a meeting. No one would have. I don't agree that her being an astronaut is what destroyed your marriage. Let's not discuss it now, please. Thanks,

Jim. I realize that you are worried. I will do my best. Love you, too. Bye." Mrs. Boyce hung up with a sigh.

Hannah rushed over and hugged her grandmother. "I'm glad we're with you, Grandma. I know we'll get home okay with you," she said. The images ran though her mind again and again. She had thrown up; her stomach was expressing her fears. What if they got trapped over here? She felt powerless to help herself or all those people who were hurt, trapped, or dead. All she wanted to do was get home, which was impossible right now.

"Mom! Thank God!" said Niki finally reaching her mother. "Yes, I should have remembered that you never stay downtown. I'm just glad that you are okay. It was scary hearing it over here and not knowing where you were. How about Dad? He's with you, right? Okay. Love you. Yes, here is Mrs. Boyce."

"Hello, Marilyn. Terrible. Yes, we should not have any trouble here in Italy. Yes, I agree, it's a beautiful country. No, I don't think we'll extend our trip and tour around; we'll monitor the airport situation on this end and get out as soon as we can. I want to get home now. The vacation joy is gone for us now.

"We'll send the luggage back to my Calistoga place as soon as we know when we can get out. Thanks for your support, dear. I'm glad that you are safe. Don't worry; you know me. I'll get them home safely. We'll keep in touch with you by email; it's more reliable. Love you, dear. Bye." Mrs. Boyce hung up again, hoping she sounded more confident than she felt.

"Hannah, I feel sick," said Niki in a whisper. "You threw up; I heard you. Listen, I'm scared, too. I mean, I like Florence, but come on, it is not California. I don't want to stay here. And what about all those people? I didn't even like looking out at the visitor platform in the World Trade Center, never mind jumping off it!" Niki started to cry again.

"I know," said Hannah starting to cry again, too. "How could they do that? How could they kill us like that? I'm so glad that our mothers didn't get killed. I feel like it is a miracle for them but still no word on Brian."

"Come here, girls. Not everyone will have a miracle today, girls. They'll get through it, but they will never get over it. Send Brian another email, and see what happens." said Mrs. Boyce. "I think we all need a hug, and then we will make a plan. We're getting out of here as soon as we can. This place is much too close to Afghanistan; we have an ocean between us and home, and who knows when the U.S. will start to bomb Afghanistan? We don't want to get stuck on this side of the border. Let's eat some sandwiches and turn in early. We have some big challenges ahead of us for tomorrow."

Chapter 6
Getting Out of Florence

The brilliant morning sun streamed into the teens' room, and the smell of bacon and toast wafted through the apartment. Both girls stumbled out of their rooms and into the kitchen.

"I understand. No flights out. Are you telling me that not one flight took off yesterday? I understand— tomorrow. I was on hold for forty-five minutes before you talked to me today!" Mrs. Boyce protested.

"Good morning, Grandma," Hannah whispered as she hugged her grandmother. "Anything else bad happen?" Hannah noticed the laptop open and the news playing across the screen. She felt sick again. Grandma never turned on the laptop, although she had a super system in her winery office and was an experienced computer user. Hannah ran over and checked her email. No response from Brian or her brother telling her what happened to Brian.

"Good morning, dear." Mrs. Boyce returned her gentle snuggle.

"Good morning, Mrs. Boyce," Niki said, giving Mrs. Boyce a hug, too. "I feel more like your very own granddaughter each day. Did I ever tell you that I love you? Well, if I haven't, I do."

"I love you, too, Niki." Mrs. Boyce smiled reassuringly at both girls. "Nothing new bad has happened, but that brave Rudy Giuliani was on TV to report updates. He was trapped himself but got out. Not only did he clean up that city, he is a real hero in this tragedy, too. You two are my favorite people in the whole world, especially right now. I can't think of any two people I'd rather be stranded in Italy with."

"What do you mean stranded?" Hannah asked worriedly.

"Well, I've been on the phone for hours this morning. I called Continental Airlines, and their telephone customer service is as useful as pumps on an elephant. I had a ninety-two-minute wait just to talk to the girl who told me that all flights into U.S. airspace have been canceled indefinitely. But last night, I decided that it's not safe here and we are going to get home. If I have to swim across the ocean, I'm going to get you girls home to your parents safely."

"Grandma!" Hannah gasped. "Swim across the ocean? Sail maybe, but swim? No way!" She giggled and hugged her grandmother again.

"Well, you know what I mean," Mrs. Boyce smiled and hugged Hannah back. "We will get home as soon as possible. The customer service person did say that she heard that flights might resume by Friday. Since we are scheduled for a Saturday flight we should probably just sit tight, and we may get out as scheduled. However, she said that airport security is going to be extra stiff, so we'd better be at the Milan airport at least four hours before our flight."

"But Grandma, I checked our tickets, and we only have a forty-five-minute layover between the Florence flight and the one in Milan. And knowing how messed up the Air Italia operations are, we will never get though the hassle in time to make the flight," said Hannah.

"Right you are again," Mrs. Boyce grinned. "That's why today we are going to head right over to that Air Italia office I saw by the Ponte Vecchio and find an alternate flight to get us to Milan on Friday instead of Saturday morning. I've already called the Hilton, and I reserved us a suite—TVs, phones, honor bar, the works."

Hannah and Niki both broke out in applause and laughter. "Oh, boy, closer to home and an honor bar," Niki laughed gleefully.

"I wonder if they have a swimming pool?" Hannah asked.

"It's hard to know what they will have in the way of amenities. This country has different services than America. Let's face it. We are spoiled. We live in the best state in the best country in the world," Mrs. Boyce commented. "I do need you two to do something for me right now."

"Anything, Grandma," Hannah smiled. "Just name it."

"Very well, I need you two to go pack up your suitcases. We're going to need to travel light, so we are going to pack up everything nonessential and ship it home via Federal Express. I've called the main office here in Florence and scheduled a pickup for 9:30 this morning. But for right now, you two are going to eat breakfast. I don't want you two to report to your parents that I starved you."

"Do I have time to shower first?" asked Niki. "I'm feeling kind of yucky, and I didn't sleep very well."

"Go ahead, if it will make you feel better. But you are not getting out of here without a nutritious meal."

"Don't you worry about that. I'm hungry, really hungry," Niki grinned and trudged off into the shower room with her robe and slipper tucked under her arm.

"I'm ready to eat right now, Grandma." Hannah pulled her grandmother's arm toward the kitchen.

"Well, so am I." Mrs. Boyce yielded to the tugging and headed with Hannah toward the kitchen.

The shower room in the apartment was a tiny converted closet. Many of the things that used to be stored in the closet were actually still there, like the vacuum cleaner that was stashed behind the shower's glass wall. "Strange place to keep a vacuum cleaner," Niki thought to herself as she shampooed her hair. Strange country, too—so friendly yet so scary. She thought about the *Godfather* movies she'd watched on rented videos with her father.

The shower itself was about the size of a postage stamp. The showerhead on the other wall was way high up on the wall and almost unreachable by the shorter girl, Hannah. Niki could stand on her tiptoes and adjust the angle of the showerhead. So when she was done showering she tilted the head of the shower toward the door, so whoever turned on the shower next would get a blast of water in the face. Niki knew that this would be Hannah, and she giggled to herself as she wrapped her space-age high-absorbency turban around her wet hair.

"Your turn, Hannah Banana," Niki yelled as she dashed from the shower room to her room to change into her clothes.

Hannah, having just gulped down two bacon-and-toast sandwiches and a glass of orange juice—no milk because milk was one of those hard to find things here in the old city of Florence—grabbed her robe and dashed into the shower room.

Niki listened intently as Hannah turned on the water. "Yeow! Niki, you, you . . . brat!" Hannah sputtered as she raced with her bathrobe soaking wet out of the shower room and into Niki's room. "Take that!" yelled Hannah as she dumped the pitcher of drinking water that was sitting on Niki's nightstand onto her freshly dried hair.

Niki could do nothing but bend over in laughter. Hannah looked like a drowned rat, and now so did Niki. They both laughed until they could not stand up. They fell to the floor and giggled uncontrollably.

Mrs. Boyce was standing in the hallway eyeing the spectacle tolerantly. "I hope this little display is simply a tension breaker. You two look really silly."

"Hannah is the real nut case around here," Niki teased.

"Oh, yeah. It's me that's the prankster? I'm sure." Hannah used Niki's head as a post to steady herself as she stood up.

"Get your hands off of me!" Niki jumped up, pushed Hannah back onto the floor, and dashed out of the bedroom to the kitchen table. "This looks great, Mrs. Boyce. You're the best," Niki said, piling bacon, toast, and fruit onto her plate.

In the meantime, Hannah had collected herself enough to get up and head back into the shower room. "I'll get you back, you know," Hannah said smugly as she restarted the shower water, more carefully this time.

"Oh, sure you will," Niki yelled back and nodded as if she just couldn't wait for Hannah to try something funny.

The next hour was full of decisions. "Should I pack this or put it in my carry-on?" was the main question. Finally, after several reorganizations, all three of the travelers had most of their belongings crammed back into the suitcases they arrived with.

"I may need a little pull cart to carry my carry-on bag," Niki laughed, looking at her overstuffed backpack.

"Me, too," Hannah said looking at her equally stuffed case.

"Not me," Mrs. Boyce said confidently. "My traveling clothes are designed to be condensed into small packages, and I also have these handy pack-mates. See, all you do is squeeze the air out of everything, and bingo it's a tiny little package."

"That is so cool, Grandma. I think I need a couple of those pack-things."

"I'll put them on your Christmas list," Mrs. Boyce said with a smile.

Just then the buzzer sounded. Hannah ran to the panel and pressed the doorbell button. "Who is it?" she asked.

"Federal Express, pickup," said a sad-sounding voice over the intercom.

Hannah pushed the button to open the door. "Come up to Apartment 1A."

They heard the front door open and the clickity click of someone's heels and a cart coming up the stairs. Hannah opened the door just as a sad-looking young man came up the stairway.

"I'm here for your pickup." He tried to smile.

"We're almost ready." Mrs. Boyce greeted him with a look of concern. "Is there something wrong, young man?"

"Oh, *Signora*, I am so unhappy about what happened in New York. The news has been devastating to my family. My uncle worked in the World Trade Center, and he hasn't been heard from. The news is bad. My family is from Afghanistan. My relatives have migrated all over the world to build new lives. We've lost so much. And now the people who are still there are in grave danger."

"I am so sorry." Mrs. Boyce looked concerned.

"Please fill out this bill of lading for me," the young man asked Mrs. Boyce, returning to the business at hand. "You need to declare the contents of the suitcases. And don't lock them. Customs will want to look inside."

"Now they tell us. If I'd known that, I wouldn't have locked up the suitcase for the trip over here," Niki reflected. "It would have been a lot less trouble for Mrs. Boyce, who had to spend hours on the phone with American Express just to get my suitcase through customs," Niki thought.

"Aren't you frightened, *Signora*? Your border is closed. You cannot get back inside. You may need these suitcases."

Hannah and Niki stared at each other with their eyes growing wide as the idea of being trapped set in.

"No, we'll get back," said Mrs. Boyce. "We're going up to Milan early to give ourselves a better chance."

"But no planes are flying. And Milan—rumors say that terrorists meet there."

"Wow, that's depressing," said Hannah.

"You got that," agreed Niki.

"You are brave, *Signora*, and with the pretty girls, too. The world is a violent place and will probably get worse."

"Why do you say that?" said Niki.

"You're stuck!" repeated the delivery guy. "The world is shut down, and you are stuck here with us in the fair country of Italy."

He loaded the suitcases into the elevator as the girls and Mrs. Boyce stepped into the hallway to help him. "Is your truck outside?" Mrs. Boyce asked him, trying to change the subject and opening the door out to the hallway.

"No. I don't have a license to park in this part of town. Federal Express doesn't have very good privileges around here. The owner must not be from Florence. I've got a hand truck, and I'm parked about fifteen blocks from here. Don't worry, I'll be careful." He tried to smile again, but Mrs. Boyce could see he was on the verge of breaking down.

"Very well." Mrs. Boyce handed him a ten-thousand-lira bill as a tip. "Thank you. Do you need us to help you with the bags on the lift?"

"Oh, no. You ladies go about your business. I'll take care of them from here. You have enough problems since you are trapped here," he answered as he put the bags on the lift, pushed the button, and headed down the steps.

"Well, girls, I am going to be blunt. We need to pull together and get home. We are vulnerable as targets, and we don't want to become victims or tools of the enemy.

"We are even more vulnerable with my minor celebrity in the wine industry that is right here in town, Hannah's mother's fame as the payload scientist who went to the space station—and Niki, let's not forget your mom the movie actress who is famous throughout the world. Other terrorists have kidnapped tourists like us to make the news, to draw attention to themselves and their cause, or to get money.

"In addition, the president may order bombing of Afghanistan, and we want to get home before that happens. Everyone I talked to is negative about our chances, but I feel we have to try to do it now. All we need are three seats to the North American continent, and we will find them! How do you feel? Now tell me the truth!"

"We want to go home! Now!" said Hannah and Niki in unison.

"Okay," said Mrs. Boyce. "Now we are going to work together as a team. We need information about the people who are getting out. How are they doing it? We will find out and just do it that way.

"I'm sorry that our vacation is over, but we'll make the most of each day as best we can. I know I can count on you. First step. Are you ready to go to the Air Italia office with me? I may need your passports to book the tickets, so I think I'd like you to come with me."

"Sure, we're not letting you go anywhere by yourself," Hannah and Niki piped in together. "Grandma, let us know what to do, and we'll do it."

It only took a few minutes for the three of them to make their last-minute preparations for the day and head out the door.

Signoria Piazza had a particularly eerie feeling about it that day. There were about as many people as usual, but everyone was a bit quieter than usual. The tour guides still led their tour groups through the plaza. But the tourists, especially the Americans, were noticeably sad and clinging to each other.

Hannah, Niki, and Mrs. Boyce made their way through the crowded streets and eventually found the Air Italia office in an alley just before the turn to the Ponte Vecchio. The office was extremely crowded with people waiting in a line that snaked chaotically out the door and into the street.

"Please just wait here in front of the window, so that once I am inside I can see you," Mrs. Boyce instructed the girls as she entered the airline office.

"Hey, Hannah?" Niki tapped the back of Hannah's hand one time very gently.

"What?" Hannah replied.

"Look over there." Niki motioned toward a little dark Middle Eastern girl, probably seven years old, who was sitting on the curb crying softly.

"I wonder what's up here," Hannah said as she walked over and knelt next to the little girl and cupped the girl's chin in her hand

"What's wrong?" asked Hannah.

The girl with a sad pout pointed toward a group of ten-year-old Italian boys who were tossing a doll dressed in a burka to each other like a rubber ball.

Hannah looked at Niki. Niki flashed Hannah the peace sign and strode confidently toward the boy with the doll. The doll's fabric flapped around as the boys continued to throw it back and forth.

Without a second's hesitation, Niki plucked the doll out of her midair flight and stuffed the doll into the pocket of her travel vest.

The boy, stunned at first, reacted like most boys would by charging straight at Niki as she walked away. Niki simply turned, and her self-defense training kicked in. With one smooth motion, Niki pulled his arm and using the energy, lurched the boy up in an arc. The boy landed with a smack on his back against the Air Italia windows. The people on line quickly turned to stare.

Niki flipped the doll through the air to Hannah. Hannah handed the doll to the little girl with the dark brown eyes, who smiled and quickly hugged Hannah and Niki.

"*Allahu Akbar*," she said as she ran off to join her friends who jumped out from their hiding place in the corner, smiling at the turn of events.

"What does that mean?" Niki asked Hannah.

"It means 'God is Great,'" replied the boy, brushing himself off as he got up.

Hannah shook her head disgustedly.

"She's one of them," said the Italian boy in perfect English.

"Oh! All nine years of her? What was she going to do to a big brave boy like you?" demanded Hannah. Niki stepped alongside her friend.

Just then a flash went off. A man nodded thanks and wrote some notes in a reporter notebook.

"Oh, no! We've been photographed!" said Niki. "Can we have it back?" asked Niki, running up to the reporter in the crumpled leather flight jacket.

"Sorry, no English," lied the reporter who disappeared down the alley.

Mrs. Boyce tapped on the window, waving at them to come in. Hannah and Niki hurried into the Air Italia office. Mrs. Boyce was finally at the front of the line. "That was a good deed, girls. I'm proud of you. I'm sure that reporter didn't recognize you."

Inside the office was a long counter with what looked like three clerks sitting at the terminals. All three of them had long brown hair pulled back into long ponytails with matching light green suits. Two of them were chatting a mile a minute in Italian and pointing at the other. The third girl was applying fingernail polish, and chewing gum with her mouth open.

"This looks a bit like a soap opera in here, Niki," Hannah remarked.

"Sure does. Let's guess which one of these gals is the evil one," Niki joked.

"They all look pretty spooky to me," Hannah answered.

"Me, too!" They both giggled nervously.

"Now, girls, be nice," Mrs. Boyce interrupted.

"Grandma, we don't want to miss a word. Please, we'll be quiet," Hannah pleaded.

"Well, then, act like ladies, and I won't have the guard over there throw you out," Mrs. Boyce replied in a friendly but firm manner.

Hannah and Niki looked in the direction that Mrs. Boyce pointed and noticed the guard asleep in his chair with his gun nearly falling out of the holster.

"OOOOh…he's scary," Hannah mugged.

"Let's hope no one attacks this place!" agreed Niki with a nervous laugh.

Mrs. Boyce sighed and approached the counter. Hannah and Niki both heard one of the girls say something like "*Americano.*"

"How can I help you today, *Signora*?" the first ticket agent asked in very clear English. Please tell me that you are extending your stay, and don't tell me that

you want to go back to America. It's impossible!"
The agent waved her hand, dramatically punctuated
by the bright red fingernails.

Mrs. Boyce pulled the tickets out of her purse. "I
want to exchange the tickets to Milan for a day
earlier, and I need to know the status of my flight into
Newark on Saturday."

"It's impossible! The earliest you will get out of here
is Saturday, and the earliest you get out of Italy is
November! You are stuck. I am sorry, but you must
accept it. Stuck. Trapped here with us! I've said it to
everyone over and over. It is not our fault! No
exceptions!"

Out of nowhere, Tony, dressed in dry-cleaned blue
jeans, an Armani white T-shirt and a short dungaree
jacket, slipped to the front of the line, which seemed
to part to let him through.

"*Signora.*" Tony took Mrs. Boyce's hand and kissed
the back of it gently as he politely bowed. "Can I be
of service to you?" He smiled charmingly.

Mrs. Boyce debated her reply, looking over at Tony.
"I've been trying to arrange a flight to Milan on
Friday and verify that our tickets to Newark are still

good. I can't seem to be able to make the arrangements with this young lady," Mrs. Boyce answered slowly.

"Evangelista!" Tony snapped at the agent.

"Yes, *Signor* Vasari, sir." Evangelista sat up straight. The other agent twisted the cap of her nail polish shut and placed it in her top drawer.

"Will you please take care of this lady and her two young wards?" Tony motioned toward Hannah and Niki who were standing nearby, all ears and paying close attention to what was going on. "They are my personal friends."

"Yes, sir, *Signor* Vasari, sir. I take care of it right away." Turning to Mrs. Boyce, Evangelista said, "Would the 11:15 flight be suitable?"

"Yes, dear, that would be fine." Mrs. Boyce sighed and smiled at Tony. "Thank you so much, Mr. Vasari. We would have been here all day if it weren't for you."

"I am glad I could be of service." Tony nodded, clicked his heels, and headed toward the door. "We have an appointment, and we must be going. I'm sure I'll be seeing you around before you depart. *Ciao.*"

"That was really nice. I am so happy we have tickets! Maybe we'll get home right on schedule!" Hannah said to Niki as they followed Mrs. Boyce out of the ticket office.

"That would be fabulous! I wonder how Tony knows Evangelista!" said Niki.

"I'm not comfortable accepting help from him, but I want to get us out of here. We have accomplished step 1."

New tickets in hand, the three travelers headed back toward Signoria Piazza.

"I'd like to take a walk across the Ponte Vecchio once more while we are right here," Mrs. Boyce said. "Would you girls like to come with me while I look for a necklace with a gold Rising Christ on a cross? If you'd rather wait here and have a Coke, that would be fine, but don't wander off anywhere," she cautioned.

"I'd like a Coke, and we will stand right around here and on the bridge so you'll always be able to see us," Hannah reassured her grandmother.

"That's right. If there's any trouble to be had, it will have to come to us," Niki joked.

"That's what I'm afraid of." Mrs. Boyce looked at the two girls sternly. "I'll only be a few minutes. Just stay right around here."

"Okay, Mrs. Boyce. I'll make sure that Hannah behaves herself." Niki grinned and shoved Hannah's shoulder so that Hannah almost fell over right into an oncoming tourist.

"Fine," Mrs. Boyce waved, ignoring the shenanigans. "I'll be right back."

Hannah and Niki bought a soft drink from the street vendor and watched Mrs. Boyce window-shop her way across the Ponte Vecchio. As she entered a store about halfway across the bridge, Hannah and Niki saw Tony go into another of the high-end jewelry shops on the bridge.

Without saying a word to each other, as if they knew what each other was thinking, Hannah and Niki sneaked up to the front window of the store that Tony had entered and slyly peered in to watch what Tony was doing.

Through the window display, they saw Tony put a huge diamond bracelet around the wrist of an older Italian teen girl with bleached blond hair. The blond put on a sparkly necklace, a bracelet, a ring, and huge dangling earrings all with many diamonds. Tony handed the sales clerk a huge wad of cash and, taking the girl's hand, swaggered out of the shop.

Hannah and Niki ducked behind a trash can, and he walked right past them without seeing them. They followed Tony and the girl into a cobblestone alley off the main street. The girl hastily ripped off the jewelry and threw it at him.

Tony coolly reached into his pocket and tossed several bills on the ground in her direction. Tony stuffed the diamond jewelry into his pockets and sauntered back toward the Palazzo Vecchio. The girl left in an obvious huff, with her heals clicking noisily on the cobblestones, in the opposite direction.

Looking at each other and bursting into giggles. Hannah and Niki said, "That was weird!" at the same time, of course.

"What the heck was that all about?" Hannah asked.

"It beats me. One minute he is so nice, and then the next minute he's being a complete Indian giver. Go figure," Niki said with a puzzled expression.

Finally, Mrs. Boyce returned to where the girls were hanging around. "Well, what's next? My mission is accomplished here." Mrs. Boyce smiled, touching her new cross that she was already wearing.

"Let's have a look at the market. I read about it in the tour book. It's called Mercato Centrale. After that we could have a look at the open-air market next to San Lorenzo Church. The book said it is geared toward tourists and sells T-shirts. I told everyone back home that I'd bring some home," Niki suggested excitedly.

"Fine with me, but remember you have already sent your suitcase out. So I wouldn't buy too many things you have to carry," Mrs. Boyce warned.

"Dang, I forgot about that," Niki said. "Let's go anyway. I'll think small for all those shirt lovers."

"I have a better idea," Hannah interjected. "Let's get lunch."

"You and your hollow leg, Hannah." Niki shook her head in disgust. "I wish I had your metabolism. If I ate like you, I'd be as big as a house."

"Just lucky, I guess," Hannah smiled.

"You bet I am lucky. You are not the first person jealous of my fantastic metabolism. Got it from Grandma. And that is not the only great thing about my grandmother."

Hannah looked at her grandmother with a new level of gratitude. "Niki is here by herself," she thought. "But I have Grandma. Grandma has taken charge and not afraid to buy her way out of here, if that is what it took. I am lucky, lucky, and lucky. I want to make sure that someday I can help someone just like Grandma is helping me."

Just then, who should stroll round the corner into the market but Eduardo, with a stunningly beautiful Italian girl on his arm.

"Hannah, Niki, *Signora* Boyce. What a pleasure it is to see you here today. I'd like you to meet Giselle, my girlfriend. She doesn't speak English very well, but as you can see it really doesn't matter, does it?" Eduardo smiled broadly.

Niki's first impulse was to knock Giselle to the ground and pull out all her hair. "Dang, she's gorgeous, even with the fake boobs," she thought. Her mother had taught her to spot them a mile away.

"Let's see if Hannah can figure it out. Have I taught her well?"

Hannah's first impulse was to run. The minute Eduardo showed up, all she could do was stammer dumb stuff like, "Nice to met yah." Hannah thought, "Just shoot me now. That girl is too gorgeous to be real. But wait a minute." She looked over at Niki, and they smiled together. "Fake boobs," thought Hannah. "At least I still have a chance for mine to grow larger." Even in this crummy situation, it was funny, and she was so glad that Niki was here.

"*Signora* Boyce, I plan to stop by the apartment about 9:00 on Saturday to pick up the key. Is that acceptable to you?" Eduardo asked.

"I'm so glad we had a chance to see you. With the terrorist attack at home, we had to change our travel plans," Mrs. Boyce explained. "We'll be leaving Florence a day early. If you could drop by on Friday morning instead, we would be very grateful. I've called Cardini to come and pick us up at 10:30."

"I'll be there around 9:45 then to return your deposit and pick up the keys," Eduardo said and then turned to Hannah and Niki. "I'm not sure if this is appropriate to suggest, but I've called my cousins

Eduardo smiled, linking his free arm around Mrs. Boyce's petite waist. "I will take you for dinner tonight, and tomorrow I will return with the cook. He will bring a small staff with him. After all, you Americans did for us during the last war, I am happy to try to help you during this terrible time." Hannah and Niki hesitantly acclimated to the concert idea with some guilt. But Eduardo, now he was something else. "He's a hunkamundo, for sure," Niki whispered to Hannah.

"You've got that one right, Niki," Hannah replied. Hannah and Niki linked arms, and they all headed toward the café for dinner.

Eduardo, Giselle, Mrs. Boyce, Hannah, and Niki talked and talked over the usual dinner of pizza Marguerite. The kind reassurances of Eduardo and proprietor of the restaurant helped to pass the time, but under the surface Hannah, Niki, and Mrs. Boyce knew that it was going to be a difficult night to fall asleep.

Chapter 7
Candlelight Ceremony on Signoria Piazza

*T*he next morning, Hannah woke with a start. Suddenly, she remembered the World Trade Center bombing and the people jumping and was afraid again. She just wanted to get home. She quickly got up and joined her grandmother, who was cooking in the kitchen. For once, Niki remained sleeping

"What are we going to wear now that we sent all of our clothes home?" wailed Hannah like a baby. "What should we do? Should we even be trying to get out early?"

They set up a late breakfast at the table overlooking the plaza. "You know, Grandma, they probably watched armies parade right here on this plaza when Florence lost to their attackers. And now we're at war again. Doesn't anything change?" she continued.

"You girls need a distraction," said Mrs. Boyce as she handed Hannah a credit card. "Go over to the Santa Croce Church. That church has the bodies of Michelangelo, Galileo, and many others. It has a fantastic energy to it—as if they are infusing everyone with that spark they used to contribute to the world.

"It is close, and it should be safe. Pick up some outfits for both of you for tonight, and you both need new carry-on luggage. Remember, it has to fit in the overhead compartment and have wheels. They will not let those carry-ons you two brought over on this time."

"Yeah, maybe Niki can drop all her stuff on that cute guy and fall in love again!" laughed Hannah.

"What's that? Hannah up before me? This is a real event!" said Niki, entering the kitchen sleepily. "Are you ever going to let me forget dropping everything on that cute guy? It was so embarrassing, but he was so nice about it. While we're on the subject, what would be wrong with seeing Peter again? He is in Milan, you know, and who knows how long we'll be there."

"You're right, Niki," said Grandma. "You have several hours before the cook gets here. It will be good for us to be with people tonight. Meanwhile, Niki, I was suggesting that you and Hannah go over to the Santa Croce Church and see the graves of some of Florence's finest. I've given her my credit card for you to get an outfit for tonight and new carry-ons for the trip back that will fit the new requirements."

"Thanks, Mrs. Boyce!" said Niki. "You are so uncomplicated about money. It will be a relief not to think about the bombing for a little while. I know those poor people in New York and Washington are thinking about it 24/7." Niki felt guilty again but pushed it back.

"My friend Annie emailed me that back home they are doing fundraisers, and some are making booties for the search dogs at the World Trade Center. I have to do something when I get home, but there is nothing to be done here right now."

"You got that right," said Hannah. "It is frustrating."

They showered and dressed in record time.

"Thanks, Grandma. Bye!" said Hannah, giving her grandmother a kiss as she grabbed a sweater and her sunglasses and pulled open the door.

They pushed and shoved each other all the way down the steps to see who could get to the bottom of the circular stairs first.

"I think we're regressing, Niki," said Hannah when they tied at the bottom.

"Well, I don't know what else to do," said Niki. "We can't help anyone from here; we're not sure how or when we're going to get home, and being a tourist is just not happening right now. That was really cool of your grandmother to let us have the dates tonight. She is fantastic. And Eduardo—he is the nicest guy in the world."

"I agree," said Hannah. "My mood swings between sadness and crying to excitement about tonight. I like music. It beats sitting in the apartment, watching that plane crash into that tower again on my laptop. I can't believe that we could not find one TV for sale here. I will never *not* appreciate America again."

"I'm scared here, too," continued Hannah. "What is with all the Ché Guevara placards posted around town here? What is wrong here that people are looking to guys like that for leadership? I forget what the trip was with Italy during the Second World War. Do you remember?"

"No," replied Niki. "I remember that they had Mussolini. Wasn't he friends with Hitler at first?"

"But then why didn't the Germans burn down the Ponte Vecchio bridge?" asked Hannah rhetorically. "Why didn't the Palazzo Vecchio get bombed—or the Duomo? I can't believe they hung Mussolini in a gas station. I feel historically impaired here. Whoever thought that history would be important?" she asked again, not expecting an answer.

"Well, let's look online for some World War II information. We don't want to be ignorant when our dates arrive! I can't wait to see what Eduardo's cousins look like. They sure have good genes. We know that!"

"I didn't know you had looked that closely at Eduardo's jeans," said Hannah. They both laughed hysterically in fun and embarrassment at the thought.

Soon they arrived at the Santa Croce Piazza. "Let's at least see what's up with this place," Hannah said, pausing to read the sign. "This used to be a swamp! The basilica was built in 1294—wow.

"Wow. Michelangelo, Machiavelli, and Dante are buried in the basilica! Let's go in real quick! I really want to see that!"

"Okay," said Niki. "But we're going to have to be quick! We don't have much time!"

They ran up the church steps but were stopped from entering by a stooped man holding a pile of fabric precariously balanced in his arms.

"No!" he said to the girls and pointed to their bare shoulders. "You cannot enter like that!" he said with a thick Italian accent.

"But this is our only chance to see it!" said Hannah, not knowing if he spoke English or not.

The man grabbed a three-foot length of green fabric with fraying edges and shoved it at Hannah. "Four hundred lira!" he said to Hannah, who glanced over at Niki.

"What a rip-off!" said Hannah. "Look at these women strutting around with their breasts hanging out, and I have on a sleeveless shirt! This is so wrong!"

Niki pulled out the money. "Who cares? Let's just pay it," said Niki. "We don't have time to waste. Hannah, put this on and go in." As they entered the church, they burst into giggles as they adjusted the fabric stylishly over and over.

"Glad I didn't spend too much time on this outfit!" Hannah said, starting to laugh uncontrollably again. It was strange. Since the bombing, she was either up or down. "Whoa! Look on the floor, Niki! These are marble casket-markers. Creepy to walk on them!" Hannah suddenly thought of Brian again. If he wasn't blown to bits, he would have a casket soon. Tears welled up in her eyes again.

"Here's Michelangelo's memorial!" said Niki. "Wow, Hannah, he walked in this church! There were so many geniuses here in this town at the same time, and many of them are buried right here in this church! We read about it in the poem 'Sepulchers' at school. I wonder what it was like back then."

"Well, like we saw at the Palazzo Vecchio, they were at war then, too," said Hannah. "Everyone wanted to take over this region, from the other Tuscany towns to Napoleon!"

"Seems like things should have improved since way back then," said Niki with a sigh. "Look at these guys watching St. Francis dying. They look as bummed as I feel about the World Trade Center."

"The look of sorrow is the same across generations, races, and religious faiths, says Grandma," replied Hannah. "It really sucks. What time is it?"

"Oh, my God!" said Niki. "It's late! We have to get going. I don't even feel like meeting these guys tonight."

"Yeah, well, we're going to, so let's get over to those shops we saw on the way in and get something to wear," replied Hannah. "Just a few days ago, we would have been really happy about it."

The brisk shopping spree had its own energy. They located a leather store and tried on coats. "That looks beautiful," said Hannah. "You should get it."

"No, that's okay," replied Niki. "Let's go and get some outfits. I couldn't wear this tonight." Wistfully, she put the buttery red-leather jacket back onto the hanger. The salesman reduced it another one hundred dollars as they left the store, but Niki thanked the man and put her hands over her ears. "Don't tempt me," she said, laughing as she left the store.

"Look at this! Italian black shirts, pants, dresses— this is too depressing. Everywhere you look!" said Hannah. "For once, give me some color!" Soon, Hannah decided on a set of olive-green Capri's, with a matching multicolored shell top and crop-cut jacket. "How does this look?" she asked Niki.

"Great," approved Niki. "I am so proud of you, venturing into matching outfits on your own. There is a beautiful face and figure in there, if you would just let it out!"

"Let it out for what?" asked Hannah. "I want to control carefully who gets to see this body. Very carefully," she said, not being able to imagine it yet.

"For now," she continued, "I'm using this color wheel to pick the colors and making sure that I don't look fat. I can't thank you and Grandma enough for making me go to that color expert. Now I just pick colors on the wheel and not waste time with stuff that looks terrible on me. I figure I'm in Italy, so I might as well try Capri's! No one from home will see me, and everyone is wearing them over here."

"Fat? That is ridiculous. You are ahead of me in the development department, as we know. I wish I had some of that extra weight, as you call it."

"The outfit has a sheer scarf that goes with it, but this is enough of a jump for now," said Hannah, ignoring the reference to her developing breasts. She wanted breasts, but she didn't like the nasty attention from creepy guys and men. She was still uncomfortable about her body. At least she was not fat like Shirley in history class.

"On second thought, since the scarf comes with it, we'll see how brave I get. I like going to other countries, because it's fun to dress up in that country's trends. Especially with Grandma's platinum card, when price is not an object! Let's see what you picked," Hannah said, stepping out of her dressing room to check it out.

"Here we go." Niki stepped out before the mirror with a grand gesture. The sky-blue pants and top made her blue eyes dazzle. The matching hand-knitted sweater was feminine and practical. Niki already had white sandals to go with it.

"You are good," said Hannah. "Shoes, too. That blue is perfect with your eyes! Your mother has taught you well. I wish my mother could teach me how to dress, but that is never going to happen. She dresses in Pendleton or Hanes, that's about it."

"Okay," Hannah continued. "We'll both look good. Let's get some earrings and get back to the apartment. I hope this cook is going to make something edible. No offense, but I'm glad we brought that San Francisco bread and crackers. But it's almost gone. Americans have improved on Italian cooking more than I can say. Good for my body size, but not my satisfaction."

"I totally agree," replied Niki, slipping out of the outfit. "I love shopping with your grandmother's credit card. We can get anything we want and not have to discuss it for a million years."

The girls rushed up to the counter to pay.

"*Bon giorno*," said Tony, suddenly right behind them. "The memorial concert, am I right? A lesser man would think that your sorrow at the recent tragedy isn't too great to prevent a new Italian outfit. I know that you sent your luggage back and did not expect to have to look more presentable for the chaplain of

Florence. Tell me Hannah, did you send that spectacular laptop back?"

"You seem to know an awful lot about us, Tony," said Niki, turning around.

With the tabloids stalking her mother periodically, Niki knew the signs of being watched, and she was getting sick of Tony showing up everywhere they went. Her mother's bodyguard had been teaching her since she was seven years old how to avoid being kidnapped and becoming an inadvertent helper in some action against her mother. Her mom's movie-star status had benefits and disadvantages. One disadvantage was becoming a fixation of whackos. Marilyn James knew that young actress who was shot in Hollywood by a criminal "fan" and had been taking precautions ever since.

"*Signorina* Niki! The Federal Express driver who picked up your suitcases just happened to mention it to me when he picked up some packages in my office at the Palazzo Vecchio. And young women of your beauty attract attention, surely you are used to that?" said Tony.

"What are you doing here?" demanded Niki, becoming more convinced that Tony was up to something that they should know about. What could it be?

"I am simply purchasing a small token of affection for my date tonight," Tony said, showing the teens beautiful diamond earrings. "With you two lovelies taken by Eduardo's cousins, I had to settle; but still, she deserves something."

"Something! That is quite a token, Tony. Are you going to marry her?" asked Hannah, signing the credit card receipt.

"Those are at least three carats each!" exclaimed Niki. She'd learned about diamonds from her mother, who had an extensive collection as investments and to wear when she appeared at premieres and award shows.

"Marriage? Oh, no! Here in Italy, we spoil our dates—unlike American boys. You have to pay for your own cheeseburger on a date. Is that correct?" said Tony. "I wish you would let me entertain you instead of Eduardo. He is so caught up in the world of fake silicon masquerading as breasts. I'm sure he does not appreciate your beauty like I do. Where is your laptop, Hannah?" asked Tony.

"It's back in the apartment," replied Hannah. "Why do you ask?"

"I am surprised you are still here in our lovely city," said Tony, ignoring her question. "Oh, that is right; you can't get home. Those mean terrorists have trapped you Americans on the wrong side of the border. Are you afraid?"

"No," said Niki. "Do you know a reason that we should be afraid?" Turn it back on the questioner, she remembered. Ask questions.

"Why, no, why do you ask? I will not keep you any longer. See you tonight!" Tony grabbed his package and exited quickly.

"Is he friend or foe? He certainly isn't stealing the diamonds talked about in the newspaper. He is buying them. But why?" wondered Hannah.

"He is really nice to us no matter who he is," Hannah continued. "I attended school with Italian, Arab, and Indian people back east, and I usually can't tell them apart. It's not like they taught it in school or anything. Can anyone tell if I am Irish, Scottish, or German? Does Tony know who your mother is? Is it a coincidence that he is everywhere we are?"

"I don't know, but it's not good. We have other choices, too, like your mother, the astronaut."

"She was a medical researcher who was a payload specialist on one mission to the space station—for the millionth time," Hannah corrected. Her mother had the white-hot light of the media on her during the preparation for her mission when the family still lived together in New Jersey before the divorce. The family was trotted out for dozens of photo opportunities. Hannah hated it. She knew that Niki had it hard in that department.

"Why is he interested in us, Niki?" she said out loud.

"I don't know, but we better get back. Let's check him out tonight at the concert," said Niki as the girls turned to go back to the apartment. When they reached the apartment, they raced to get ready for dinner.

Ding dong!

"I'll get it," said Niki, smoothing down her blouse unnecessarily and making one last check in the antique mirror mounted next to the door.

"Not bad," she said. It was cool to dress just the way she liked without the tips from her mom. She loved her mom, but it wasn't easy knowing she would never look that good. But here she felt good. Mrs. Boyce really liked her just the way she is, and this outfit would make anyone look good. So, not bad, and let's go!

"That figures. You are ready and right there to answer the door!" said Hannah, hurrying as fast as she could.

There was a certain comfort in knowing that she would not look as spectacular as Niki, but she didn't have to look like a total dork either. Hannah pushed her curly hair over one ear and jammed the thirty-dollar tortoise hair clip in to keep it back. It seemed wrong to be going to a concert when all those people were missing and the rest were in mourning. But what was she going to do, hang out here in her room and be "Hannah sullen," as her aunt called it? Hannah put a little more mascara on, threw the applicator on the ornate dresser, took a deep breath and entered the night's activities.

"Hannah, the Italian style suits you!" said Mrs. Boyce embarrassingly as Hannah entered the living room.

"Hannah, I'd like you to meet Carlo and Enrico, my cousins," said Eduardo, dressed in a red turtleneck and black pants nodding toward two handsome

Italian teenagers but closer to twenty. Both guys were total Italian hunks.

Niki squeezed Hannah's hand behind the end table and Hannah squeezed back.

"How nice is Eduardo!" whispered Hannah to Niki.

"And of course, the chaplain of Florence, Father Noran." The gray-haired man with a Roman collar, black shirt, and black pants walked over to Mrs. Boyce and shook her hand.

"I'm delighted to make your acquaintance *Signora* Boyce," said the priest. "Your reputation as a master of Chardonnay precedes you."

"My cousin Carlo is the third generation glass blower. His family has owned their shop on the Ponte Vecchio since the 1800s," said Eduardo. "Carlo made you these beautiful candle holders for you to remember us, so you know that we Italians stand with you—that we don't forget that the United States got the Nazis out of our country. Without you Americans, I don't know what would have happened."

Carlo was tall and graceful with long full hair pulled back with a yellow cloth band. He had on a yellow cashmere sweater and faded jeans with Italian leather sandals. Carlo stepped up and handed Niki a beautiful rose-colored glass with a small candle and an American flag etched in the glass.

"I am so sorry to hear about your tragedy," said Carlo handing Niki her glass. "I made these personally for you for the candlelight ceremony tonight. Please keep it as a token of our sorrow for the tragedy. The candle," said Carlo, slipping a candle into the glass, "is a sign of light and hope for the future."

The chaplain handed a lavender one to Mrs. Boyce.

"How thoughtful," said Mrs. Boyce and wiped away a quick tear.

"This is Enrico, Hannah," said Eduardo. "Enrico is in pre-law. He is the rebel. All of his people have been doctors but Enrico; he has insisted on law."

Enrico was just short of six feet and had on a black blazer, white silk T-shirt, and black pants with Italian loafers and no socks. Hannah could see him arguing a case in front of a jury. His dark black hair was parted on the side and brushed back just touching the tip of his collar.

Enrico stepped up to Hannah. "I am so sorry to hear about your tragedy," said Enrico, handing Hannah a pale-green version. "We will use these in the candlelight ceremony tonight. Please keep it as a token of our sorrow for the tragedy."

"Thank you," stammered Hannah, studying the beautiful glass with wonder. The swirls in the glass were light and delicate and seemed to hug the glass. "That is so nice!" she thought. She fought back tears. She didn't want to cry in front of people that she didn't know.

"It's beautiful. Thank you, Enrico. Nice to meet you, Carlo and Father Noran, and always wonderful to see you, Eduardo," said Hannah with her best smile. She felt like she did okay. She looked over to see Grandma beam with pride.

Enrico took Hannah's hand gently, and they walked into the living room, which had been transformed. Candles were everywhere; there were no electric lights on. The big farm table had a blue-and-yellow flowered tablecloth on it and was pulled in front of the huge window overlooking the plaza. The windows were open, and the curtains fluttered gently.

Outside, the stage was set up and ready for the concert and candlelight ceremony later.

"Excuse me for a minute," Hannah said quickly and ran back to the bedroom and retrieved some tissues for her purse. If she was going to cry, she better be prepared. The last time she was crying this much was when her parents announced the divorce. She returned to the room.

"Let's all eat," said Mrs. Boyce.

"This looks fantabulous!" said Niki sitting down. There were fresh fruit, big bowls of salad, eggplant Parmesan, veal Parmesan, fettuccine, and garlic bread.

Father Noran was a charmer who regaled everyone with stories of World War II throughout dinner. When the delicious dinner was finished, the chaplain paused from a story and said, "It is your turn now, young people. You have a different kind of evil and some right here in this town! In any case, it is time for you to get down to the ceremony. We'll stay here and watch from the window."

Hannah, Enrico, Niki, and Carlo joined the people in the plaza. Tourists and locals, all ages, shapes, and sizes, packed the plaza. The firefighters from all the surrounding towns in Tuscany—Siena, Assisi, and Pisa—were all lining the edges of the stage. Firefighters started coming through the crowd to light everyone's candles. The mood was somber but close.

Niki nudged Hannah. "There's Tony," said Niki pointing to Tony on stage. "Let's see if we can find anything in his office in the Palazzo Vecchio," said Niki. "It's right through that door, and he is obviously occupied."

"Do you know him?" asked Enrico with alarm. "There are many rumors about him here in town. I hope you girls stay away from him."

"What are the rumors?" asked Niki.

"He hangs around our criminals, the—how do you Americans call it—the fences. They say he has purchased many diamonds."

"We saw him purchase diamonds twice," said Hannah. "Once at Santa Croce Piazza and the other time at Ponte Vecchio!"

"See, he purchases many diamonds, but we don't know what for," agreed Enrico. Hannah could tell he was going to make a great lawyer. "Investigators here believe that some terrorists are buying diamonds to smuggle into the United States to finance more terrorist attacks!"

"Why don't they just use regular money?" asked Hannah.

"Because they cannot exchange large amounts of money without arousing suspicion," said Enrico. "Anything above ten thousand dollars must be reported by the bank to authorities in your country. But you can sell the diamonds for local currency without it being traced. You cannot trace diamonds anywhere in the world so criminals use them as currency."

"I have to go use the ladies' room," said Hannah suddenly. "Niki, come back with me, please?"

"Yes, you two go together, and stay away from Tony," said Carlo.

"Don't worry!" said Hannah.

Niki and Hannah darted down the hall right by the bathrooms. There was a light in Tony's office. Niki knocked on the door—no answer. Hannah pushed lightly on the door, and it opened.

"Sweet," said Hannah. They crept into the office.

"What are we looking for?" asked Niki.

"I don't know. Just look," replied Hannah.

"Look at this! It's the statue of the three-headed dragon," said Niki. "I'm going to take a picture of it." Niki snapped a picture with a digital camera. The flash flooded the room with light.

"Yikes! I hope no one saw that flash," said Hannah. "What's up with that three-headed dragon? I'm sure he doesn't leave diamonds lying around in here. Let's get back to the ceremony. I don't want to miss it."

Just then the door slammed loudly, and they heard the lock click.

"Oh, no!" said Hannah running over to the door and twisting the doorknob rapidly.

"It's locked! Grandma is going to kill us!"

"Grandma kill us?" replied Niki with alarm. "I don't think that's who we should be worried about. We've got to get out of here quick!"

Hannah unclipped her mini-flashlight from her long necklace and shined it around the room. The three-headed dragon's shadow seemed to climb up the wall from the desk and hover over them menacingly.

Niki tried the door again and threw her body against the huge mahogany door. "Ow!" said Niki when the door didn't budge. "We're not getting out that way!"

The brass band started playing "America the Beautiful" outside, which drowned out Niki pounding on the door.

"No one will hear us either," said Niki, "and we're missing the ceremony!" she cried. "This was so stupid getting caught in here, and we haven't even picked up a clue!"

"Who locked us in here?"

"Tony probably. I wonder if he knows we are in here. How embarrassing."

"Who cares?" asked Niki. "Let's try the window."

They rushed over behind the desk and pushed up on the massive stained-glass window.

"Can we bear to break fifteenth-century glass?" asked Niki sadly.

"That might be better than getting caught in here by anyone else. Who knows who locked us in here? I hope Grandma doesn't know we're gone yet."

"Well, I don't think that Eduardo ran up to the apartment to tell her he lost us!

We probably have some time."

"Okay." Hannah jumped up on the desk, ran her hand over the top of the window, and flicked a lever. "Now try it, Niki!"

"It opened!" said Niki excitedly.

"Shine your flashlight down there, and see how far the drop is."

Hannah shined the flashlight. "I think we can do it. There's ivy growing up the wall! It's only one story down."

"We're not dressed for it, but let's go for it," agreed Niki climbing up onto the windowsill. Immediately, she fell onto the floor. She looked up and they both burst out laughing.

Suddenly they heard footsteps outside on the marble floor.

"Hurry! Hurry! You go out first," said Niki moving back.

Hannah hopped out the window and grabbed onto the ivy on the first lunge. The ivy fell away from the building, and Hannah started to free-fall. She grabbed at new strands and fell away like she was rappelling down the building in an awkward but effective way.

"They're coming in the door, Hannah! Quick, get out of my way!"

Niki looked down at Hannah almost falling but hopped out anyway.

Hannah looked up just in time to see a huge arm reach out and grab Niki around the neck. "Watch out," yelled Hannah in a panic.

Hannah continued down the ivy, grasping at the leaves as the branches scratched her arms when she fell finally to the cobblestone walkway below with a smack.

"Ow!" said Hannah, feeling the tears of pain instantly running down her cheeks.

"Help! Help!" shouted Niki, gasping for breath. "Let go of me!" said Niki, turning as she grabbed at the ivy trying to get away from the guy.

Hannah struggled to get up. The back of her head throbbed.

Niki lurched down the ivy, but the man refused to let go. He shouted in Italian back into the room. Niki was choking. Hannah started back up the ivy to help.

Suddenly, Niki's jacket ripped, and the man lost his grip. Instantly Niki fell on top of Hannah, and they both collapsed onto the cobblestones.

Hannah rolled over, got up, and stared up at the window.

"Get them!" yelled the man in the window with a thick Italian accent.

Niki gulped and gulped again, grasping her throat, trying to catch her breath. She finally heaved in a breath and stumbled to her feet.

"Let's go," she said, grabbing Hannah's hand to pull her along and automatically brushing dirt and ivy from her hair.

Hannah and Niki ran alongside the massive building to rejoin the ceremony. It took them a few minutes to find their dates and Eduardo.

"Where have you been?" asked Carlo with a worried look. "You didn't follow Tony did you? He disappeared right after you two went to the ladies' room. He didn't follow you, did he?"

"There was a long line," replied Niki lamely.

"How did you get that ivy in your shoe while you were in the bathroom? What happened to your arms; they are all scratched! Tell us! What happened? Did someone harm you? We will make them pay!" said Enrico.

"We were trying to find clues in Tony's office. It's our fault. We didn't find anything either!" said Hannah. "We jumped out the window when we got caught. They choked Niki, and then her jacket ripped!" Hannah pointed to Niki's ripped jacket.

"They are dangerous!" said Enrico. "We've been trying to get proof of Tony's criminal activity for months. You are lucky you did not get hurt!"

"Could you identify them?" asked Enrico.

"Dark hair, big arms, that's it!" said Hannah.

Just then, the sexy rock star opened the second half of the show with a sad song about life's opportunities lost. People from the community and each city spoke. Hannah and Niki were crying as they watched the horrible videos playing on the huge screen behind the stage. It was just heartbreaking. The band played "God Bless America," and Niki and Hannah sang from the bottom of their hearts with everyone else. A middle-aged Italian couple gave them each a hug and apologized. Everyone seemed to be asking, "Why?" But no one had an answer.

Hannah looked up to see her grandmother and the priest waving to them to come in from the window. "We better go," said Niki.

Enrico swept Hannah into his arms "You are a very brave girl, Hannah, and I will never forget you. Email me, and let me know that you got home safely."

"Bye, you guys, it was great," said Hannah suddenly feeling comfortable now that it was too late.

"Look, your poor arms. Take my jacket with you to warm you, and know that a humble Italian cares for you," said Enrico, placing Hannah's arms in his silk jacket.

Carlo gently placed his sweater over Niki. "Yes, Niki, take my sweater. You are brave girls, but be careful! You face a dangerous trip home. Do not trust anyone."

By this time, they were at the apartment-building door. Hannah turned the key in the lock—they held each other's hands and ran up the stairs with the sweater and jacket wrapped tightly around them.

Chapter 8
Milan Getaway

"Did you girls sleep?" asked Mrs. Boyce as the girls stumbled into the kitchen the next morning, already dressed for the long trip.

"Not really," said Hannah.

"Me neither," said Niki.

"What a wonderful evening against a backdrop of tragedy and sadness," said Mrs. Boyce.

"I'm going to try and log on once more before we go," said Hannah. It was getting harder each day to pretend that Brian was going to be found alive. No email from Brian. Just an email from Jimmy who said that Brian's sister made a poster with his picture asking people to call if they found him and taped it in all the New York hospitals. Hannah wiped away a tear and snapped the laptop shut for the journey.

Niki walked over to the window. "Hannah, just a few days ago, we were filled with joy; now we have to leave, and I'm afraid that we might not get home!"

"I know," said Hannah giving her a hug.

"We have strong shoulders, and we will make the best of it, girls," said Mrs. Boyce sipping her second cup of coffee. The door buzzer rang twice quickly. "That's Eduardo now," she remarked as she brushed the tablecloth quickly to straighten it out and headed toward the door. Hannah beat her to the button.

"Is that you, Eduardo?" Hannah asked into the intercom.

"Yes, it's me," Eduardo responded cheerfully.

Hannah pushed the entry button and took a quick look in the mirror. "Not too bad," she thought. "Grandma says excitement brings out the highlights in my hair."

Eduardo stepped through the door with his usual self-confident stride.

"He always looks like a million bucks," Niki commented quietly to Hannah.

"More like a hundred million lira," Hannah replied with a giggle.

Both girls nodded in agreement. He was a hunk. Mrs. Boyce and Eduardo settled up the balance as the girls rushed around stuffing their last-minute items into their already bursting carry-on bags.

"Well, Eduardo, as you can see, Cardini hasn't arrived yet. I'm a little concerned. I'm going to call the travel agent and check up on him."

"Traffic is very bad this morning. If he's stuck somewhere, he may be way too late to take you to the airport. I have my car if you need me."

"Eduardo, that is very nice of you. I have a funny feeling about Cardini."

Mrs. Boyce left the living room and went into her room to make her call. She was back in a short minute. "Well, Eduardo, I think we will have to take you up on your offer. Cardini is not only stuck in traffic, he's nowhere to be found."

"Well, ladies, let's get these bags into the lift and be on our way. Traffic is heavy, but the airport isn't far." Eduardo smiled and opened the door to the apartment.

When all the bags were down on the lift and out the front door, Niki asked, "Where are you parked, Eduardo? The Federal Express driver had to hike in fifteen blocks; you know, no cars and all that."

"Well, I've got a parking permit on my car. Since we own our apartment, we can park for short periods of time. Usually not during the day however. And I've been here for more than a half-hour. If you see any of the police officers looking at my car, try to distract them until I can get your bags into the boot and we can get out of here."

The suitcases safely tucked into the trunk, Hannah and Niki climbed into the tiny back seat, and Mrs. Boyce got the shotgun seat. Hannah and Niki heard Mrs. Boyce gasp as Eduardo proceeded to break every traffic law ever written. He ignored stop signs and made illegal U-turns about four times. "I should have sat in the front," Hannah remarked quietly to Niki. "Grandma is a little sensitive and gets nervous. I see she's doing her best not to clutch the dashboard, but look at her white knuckles."

After the brief but thrilling trip to the airport, Eduardo pointed in the direction of the tiny outbound terminal and kissed them all goodbye. "It has been wonderful having you here, and I will always remember your visit. Please come back again soon."

"Thank you, Eduardo." Mrs. Boyce hugged him firmly. "You have made our visit very memorable as well. We will come back and see you . . . soon. Or, you could come and see us. Our Second Rising Ranch is so much like Tuscany; you will feel right at home."

They all waved and headed toward the terminal. They flew the quick flight to Milan and entered the terminal expectantly. Thousands of people, animals, and pieces of luggage were packed into the terminal.

"Oh, my God!" said Hannah disappointed. "Are all these people trying to get out of here?"

"That's right," said a harried father dragging a little boy toward the restroom with a waiting line of twenty guys stretching outside the door and into the terminal.

"Let's check the Continental Airlines counter and see
if we can get any information about tomorrow's
flight," Mrs. Boyce said as they walked through the
Milan terminal.

"Okay," Hannah said, looking back over her shoulder
as she started to dash toward the Continental counter.
Bam! Hannah slammed headlong into a very tall, very
beautiful young woman.

Thud. They both fell to the floor in a heap. "Oh, my
God, you're the model on this month's cover of
People Teen," Hannah stammered.

"Well, yes, I am," The model, Helen Stanton, smiled
through her messed up head of gorgeous hair. "And
who are you?"

"I'm Hannah Jordan. I'm so sorry. I didn't mean to
knock you down. I wasn't looking where I was going.
I'm so, so sorry," Hannah repeated herself as she
helped the lanky model to her feet.

"I think I'm okay, but what's the big hurry?" Helen
asked.

"We're going over to the Continental counter to
check on our flight," Hannah said.

"Well, don't bother. The Continental counter is closed and has been all day," Helen continued. "I'm a Continental Platinum member, and I've been trying to get out of here since Wednesday. And I'm still here. All the flights have been canceled, and Continental has been absolutely unhelpful to me."

"Haven't they tried to find you alternate transportation?" Mrs. Boyce asked.

"Not so far. I would just like to get home to family. I was scheduled to go home next week. When the disaster happened, I checked out of the hotel and came right to the airport. I've been trying to get a ticket home for four days. I'm going to go back to the fashion show again today and spend another night at the Hilton. They've been gouging me, but what choice do I have. It's sleep there or sleep here." She looked around with disbelief. "Here is not good for beauty rest. And girls, have you done any runway work?"

"Gag," Niki said quietly to Hannah.

"Not me. That's for the beautiful people," Hannah blushed.

"With all the flights grounded from the U.S.A., most of the runway models that were scheduled to do the shows here can't get here," said Helen. "The show managers and designers are desperate to find people for the Milan show. You are just the right size. Are you sure you have never done runway before?"

"Where's the fashion show being held?" Niki asked, trying to change the subject.

"It's at the Jolly Hotel. Funny name, but it's a very swanky hotel. It will be completely over tomorrow, and I was hoping that I'd be able to get home. My dog is about to have puppies, and I'm not there," she mocked pouting. "The vet says she's fine, but I want to be there."

"What kind of dog?" Hannah asked.

"She's a Carne terrier. You know, like the dog Toto in *The Wizard of Oz*," Helen replied.

"Oh, how cute," both girls cooed.

"Well, if you won't substitute, here are some tickets. If you have a chance, come over to the show, and say hi," Helen said as she walked away.

"Will do," Niki said waving goodbye.

When Mrs. Boyce and the girls arrived at the Continental counter, sure enough, it was closed. A large piece of white paper was taped to the counter that said "No flights out today. This counter is closed. 800-555-1234 for more information."

I'm calling that number right now," Mrs. Boyce said, dialing the number on the sign. "I would like to check on fight 345 from Milan to Newark tomorrow. Well, that's great. Four hours early. Okay. Great. Thank you. Bye."

"Well, girls, according to the person I just talked with, we are very lucky ladies. Our flight will take off as scheduled," Mrs. Boyce smiled. "She also said you should check the Continental Web site later today and see if there are any updates. But between now and tomorrow morning there is nothing further that we can do. Let's get over to the Hilton. I'd like to rest a bit."

"That's sound great. Let's go find a cab," Hannah started toward the front door of the terminal.

"Wait," Mrs. Boyce said when they were nearly out the front door. "I see something interesting."

The girls followed Mrs. Boyce toward a counter labeled "Limo."

"Limo . . . hmmm, almost my favorite word right now," Niki joked.

Mrs. Boyce negotiated a deal for cash and got a discount on a Limo ride to the Hilton. She also arranged for the driver to pick them up the next morning.

"There, all taken care of, and no cabs for us tomorrow, either." Mrs. Boyce ushered the girls out the door after the driver, who led them to a Mercedes limo sitting at the curb.

The ride into Milan was uneventful. It was raining, so Hannah and Niki contented themselves with chatting about their encounter with Helen Stanton, supermodel, and giggling over how messed up her hair got.

At the Hilton, the lobby was nearly deserted, so it only took a few minutes to check in and get up to the business suite that Mrs. Boyce had secured.

"I'm going to take a real bath and a nap before dinner. I hope you two can entertain yourselves for a few hours while I relax." Mrs. Boyce hugged Hannah around the shoulders. Then Mrs. Boyce smiled and waved as she went into her room for her bath.

Turning on the TV, Hannah and Niki settled into chowing down on the contents of the mini-bar in the room. "I think I saw a convenience store in the lobby. Did you, Hannah?" Niki asked as Hannah finished off the last of the candy bar she picked for her snack.

"I'm not sure. Why don't we go have a look?" Hannah said. "Let me just go change my shoes."

"Me, too," Niki said, pushing past Hannah through the doorway into their bedroom. Niki leapfrogged over Hannah, did a somersault across her bed and landed standing upright at the foot of her bed and in front of the mirror on the dresser. With five quick strokes, she brushed her hair. Then she hopped into her walking shoes, jumped over both of the twin beds, and ended up standing in front of the door completely ready to go before Hannah had even laced up one of her shoes.

The girls stepped off the elevator and began to look around the deserted hotel lobby.

"Creepy," said Niki. "Where is everyone? There doesn't seem to be any shop in the lobby," Niki said, "like in the hotels in California."

"This is Italy. Remember, Niki? Italy! All of the conveniences of the fifteenth century. I am so bored. I wonder how long we are going to be stuck here," Hannah shrugged.

The sign "Personalized Tours" caught their eyes at the same time.

"Should we go ask your grandmother if we can go on a tour?" Niki asked Hannah.

"I don't think she'd like to be disturbed right now," Hannah said mischievously. "She did say we should entertain ourselves for a few hours. Didn't she?"

They approached the uniformed man sitting behind the desk.

"We'd like to take a tour of Milan, please," Hannah said.

"Why take a tour," said cute Peter from the plane, stepping up to the counter, "Helen Stanton told me she saw you in the airport. I'd be happy to show you around. I just came back from the show setup. Lots of the models are staying here at the hotel. The prices have gone up each night since 9/11. They know they have the models trapped here. Some people are staying 100 miles from the airport and driving in each day to try and get a flight out. We should be okay unless the terrorists do something here. Then we're really messed up. I have some time. Let me give you a tour, and we can stop by the show!"

"Hannah, this is great. Of course, your grandmother wouldn't mind us going on a tour with Peter. She knows him already. This is perfect," said Niki.

"I'll show you the Milan highlights. We'll stop by Leonardo da Vinci's *Last Supper*," Peter explained with a smile. "Let's go. My car is right outside," Peter said as he headed out the revolving door. The two girls piled into the back seat of the Mercedes.

"Company car," Peter explained.

"Niki," Hannah jabbed Niki in the ribs with her finger, "got ya back." She laughed. "Look at that." Hannah pointed toward the dashboard of the car. "Isn't that the same three-headed dragon we saw last night in Tony's office?"

"I think it is, Hannah," Niki said. "Either it's a trendy dragon club or we'd better be careful. We better be careful, but it sure feels good to be exploring. We have a long trip ahead of us, and we don't even know if that flight is going to take off tomorrow."

"I think the being-careful advice is the one we should follow," Niki added. "I have a funny feeling about Peter."

"I've been reading about what happened in New York and watching it on TV. Quite a mess," he commented. "I was a student in New York on a student visa. Now, I'm over here to study design and earn a little money. I intend to return to New York when I have enough saved."

"We're from California, but Hannah's mother works in New York. She's okay. Have you heard the rumor that Congress wants to have all student visas terminated? It seems that some people come to the U.S. to study, get in on a student visa, and disappear."

"Well," Peter stammered and then added softly, "The United States is supposed to be free, and now they are going to shut down student visas?" He turned toward the road and concentrated on his driving.

"You know, Peter," Niki added, "the U.S. doesn't need to be open so terrorists can come in and attack us! Why do they hate us so much?"

"The United States needs to review its foreign policy," replied Peter. "What are you doing in Saudi Arabia? The United States thinks it's been in charge forever, but if you will review history, you'll see that Muslims controlled parts of Europe and Asia until this century. They controlled it for longer than the United States has been a country!"

"Stop being so serious, you two," said Niki, not liking the tone of the conversation.

They soon arrived at *The Last Supper*, but it was too crowded to get in.

"Let's just go to the fashion show. It is raining anyway."

"Niki, you could be a model in your own right. I understand you are the daughter of Marilyn James," stated Peter.

"Understand from who?" asked Niki warily.

"I saw your picture when you did that show with your mother last year," replied Peter. "Why, what is the big deal?"

"No big deal," replied Niki.

"Look, let's go to the show, and you can escape this for an hour," said Peter. "Helen said she gave you tickets and put your names on the list so you can get in."

"Okay," said Hannah. "We have about two hours before my grandmother would miss us."

"We have plenty of time for fear and worry tomorrow when we try to get home," agreed Niki. "I don't want to watch those planes crash into the towers one more time. It is sickening."

"So, Peter, now that we are buddies, have you ever seen the three-headed dragon?"

"Yeah, I've seen it at the offices at a mosque in Milan. I snuck in there once with a banker who attended the show.

"Some of the guys have gold rings with that insignia, too. No one knows what it means. But two of the guys I met with the rings at the mosque were arrested on 9/11, and no one has seen them since."

Just as they arrived on the corner, a huge black limo pulled up to the curb, and the rear door flung open. The crowd pressed in toward the open door, and the limo driver shooed people away. Hannah and Niki ducked beneath the swing of his arm and peered into the open limo. Just then a long slender leg with calf-length snakeskin boot emerged from the back seat of the limo. Shortly after, the second, equally as thin, leg emerged from the limo followed by the rest of a very skinny girl.

"She looks familiar," Niki said. "Oh, my God, it's Helen Stanton. She looks so different with all that makeup on."

"Helen, Helen, it's Niki and Hannah," Niki yelled.

Helen looked around and, when her eyes met Niki's, she smiled a huge "thank God it's you" kind of smile.

"Niki, Hannah, I can't believe it's you. My manager is having a nervous breakdown. An entire crew of models got stuck in the Caribbean. They were on the *Sports Illustrated* swimsuit shoot, and their plane was grounded. We need you two right now."

"Let's go in. The show is about to start, and I have a runway slot at 2:30."

Hannah gasped. "Oh, no, not me. I'm no runway model."

Niki laughed. "Hannah, you are just as good looking as any model."

"Sure," Hannah grimaced. "Niki, you hate modeling. You've said so a million times," said Hannah starting to feel pulled where she did not want to go.

"I saw you with your Mom last year in the mother-daughter show for the Pediatric AIDS event when I was there with my mom! You were great. Be a pal!" Helen declared.

Finally Niki just gave in. "This will be good experience for Hannah," Niki thought to herself, trying to justify getting up on a runway and doing something she swore that she hated.

"It will only take a half-hour. When are we going to get a chance like this again? If Peter can take us back to the hotel."

"I'd be delighted," said Peter.

Helen handed Peter a ticket. "Here you go, Peter— front row, right next to all the celebs."

Peter headed out to the show. "I'll pick you up right after the finale."

"Let's just go in and see what Hal has to say. He was on the phone earlier, and I know he's at least five girls short."

Helen grabbed Niki's arm and shoved her. Niki grabbed Hannah's arm and dragged her along into the building, following right on Helen's heels.

"Girls, girls, attention everyone." The stage manager was frantically gathering the large group of models into a bunch. "We're running a bit behind schedule right now, so everyone will have to get changed and into position quickly. Helen, I see you've brought along some reinforcements. Very nice," she said, looking Niki and Hannah over quickly.

"Joe," the stage manager barked, "Give Curly Top here Kate's set of clothes. Curly will look marvelous in the blue silk evening pants set. Blondie here will look good in the blue taffeta and the black leather trench coat. Now, off with you all. Change, and see Bert for hair and makeup."

"I wonder who Kate is?" Hannah asked.

"Whoever she is, she's stuck in New York and can't get out. No flights, remember," Helen said leading the girls to the dressing room.

"Kate. I'm no Kate. Whoever she is, she's a . . . a . . . a . . . twig," Hannah stammered.

"Just put on the dress, and smile," Niki smiled. "You are much better than any Kate. You are a real, live, breathing, eating woman. You are beautiful."

Hannah took a huge deep breath and entered the dressing room, expecting the worst. Instead she found a group of really normal-looking girls stuffing themselves into odd-looking designer clothes.

Hannah and Niki were fortunate, because the stage manager had picked out clothes that actually looked good on them. The outfit fit Hannah to a tee, and the jacket looked like it was made for her.

Bert, the hairdresser and makeup guy, raved over Hannah's luscious curls and twisted her hair neatly behind her ears before putting a dramatic wide brim hat that dipped mysteriously over Hannah's left eye. Hannah stared at the smoky look of the eye makeup. "Your beauty is now at the front!" exclaimed Bert.

He applied the final pat of powder to her nose. "Now go! Go! Go!"

"Can I get a picture of myself like this?" asked Hannah. "No one will believe this!" Hannah posed with as wide a smile as she dared.

Bert pulled out a Polaroid from the vanity's drawer, snapped a picture, and gave it to Hannah.

"Cool!" Hannah thought as she was pushed toward the runway.

Niki's first outfit was a light blue taffeta evening dress. The one-shoulder gown flowed over Niki in a most becoming billow of taffeta, and the chiffon shawl draped over her uncovered shoulder complemented Niki's eyes. Soon, with the hair and makeup touches that were artfully applied by the makeup lady, Niki looked stunning.

"Are you ready?" asked the stage manager motioning toward Hannah, Niki, and Helen. "You are in the second set. Remember, the camera is on your left, and the show is live. So that means, no tripping, no falling, no laughing. You may smile because you are young and beautiful. Chin up, chest out. Boobs are in, and you look great." She pointed to the steps that led to the stage.

"Now," Helen looked seriously at Hannah and Niki. "Here's the deal. It's not real hard. Go up the steps. Wait at the top until the person in front of you is halfway down the runway, and then just start. Walk to the end of the runway. Pose like this." Helen struck a stunning model's pose. "Turn around, and walk back. Change quickly, and do it again. Then we all line up, and, when the last model has finished, we all go back on stage for a final walk down the runway."

"I can't believe I'm really doing this," Hannah whispered urgently to Niki as they got in line after Helen.

"You are going to be great," Niki reassured Hannah. "You look great in that outfit, and all we have to do is walk and smile."

"Yeah. That's what I'm afraid of...the walking part," Hannah sighed.

"Don't worry about it. Just follow me. Do what I do, and try to relax. Don't try too hard. Walk, smile and have fun. Remember, it's only the whole world looking at us. This show is being broadcast live."

Hannah didn't have any more time to worry about the whole thing. Before she knew it, Niki was off down the runway. "She looks completely at home out there," Hannah thought to herself.

Then it was her turn, so she just stepped out, pretending to be completely confident.

Back at the hotel, Mrs. Boyce awakened from a nap and, before checking on the girls, she decided to see what was on the television. On the Italian Fashion channel, what did she happen to see? Hannah and Niki were walking down the runway in designer clothes!

"Oh, my goodness," Mrs. Boyce said as she leaned forward to make sure her eyes weren't playing tricks on her. "That is Hannah and Niki. I just can't believe it. I tell them to entertain themselves for a couple of hours, and they end up in a designer fashion show."

"Hey! That wasn't that bad!" said Hannah to Niki as they were pushed back behind the curtain.

"You did great!" said Niki excitedly.

Ring ring!

"Whose phone is that?" demanded the stage manager. "Get it now! Turn it off!"

Ring ring!

The stage manager ran over to Hannah's day pack and pulled out her Italian cell phone, answered the phone, and threw it to Hannah.

"Hannah, is that you on TV?" asked Mrs. Boyce. "I thought I just saw you and Niki on TV! You looked wonderful dear—Niki, too!"

"Hi, Grandma! You said to amuse ourselves, right?" she said hesitantly, not sure if she was in trouble.

"I can see you are doing just that! It was wonderful to see your beautiful smile!" said Mrs. Boyce. "Make sure you come straight back when the show is over. See if you can get the stage manager's name so we can get a copy of the tape."

"Okay, Grandma. You're great!" said Hannah, giving Niki the okay sign and hanging up.

All too soon, Hannah and Niki stood on stage for the finale with the silver-haired designer with the dark tan. As the crowd cheered, Peter jumped up and led them back to the car. After briefing Mrs. Boyce on their adventure, they had a quick dinner and collapsed into bed.

Chapter 9
Canceled Flights in Milan

"**O**kay, we completed step one of getting back home; now we get on this plane to Newark, and we'll be back in the U.S.A. I'm proud of you girls getting up and out by 4:30 AM, especially after your TV appearance and all," said Mrs. Boyce the next morning as they exited the Mercedes limousine into the Milan airport.

"Oh, my gosh, Grandma, this place is packed again! That can't be good," said Hannah nervously. Hannah pressed the gold cross around her neck instinctively.

"As my Mom would say, 'What are we pretending not to know?'" said Niki, quickly assessing the airport status. Niki was a seasoned air traveler. From the time she was an infant, she traveled with her mom to different movie sets.

"These people have not left the airport," continued Niki. "They are so desperate that they didn't go to a hotel last night. They stayed here to be on standby for every flight until they can get out. That is what happened during Desert Storm, too. I don't remember it, but Mom told me that she was on location in Spain and she just wanted to go home. But she could not get out. She had to buy new tickets and everything."

"Hopefully we won't have to," said Mrs. Boyce. "But we will pay whatever it takes to get out of here today. The Web site said our plane was leaving. Let's go down and see what the story is at the Continental counter." Mrs. Boyce and the girls pulled up the handles on their new carry-on bags and began to roll them.

"Thanks for the new leather carry-on, Grandma; this makes it so much easier. I love that we got it in Florence," said Hannah more brightly than she felt.

"Me, too!" said Niki "Thanks, Mrs. Boyce."

"Oh, no," said Hannah as they rounded the corner to the Continental ticket counter.

"About a hundred and fifty people ahead of us at 5:15 AM," said Niki with that sinking inflection in her voice.

"It's canceled!" said a chubby woman in tears running up to them. "My son logged on in the U.S. and told us. This is our third day here. We're never going to get out of here! What if the U.S. starts bombing Afghanistan? We'll never get out of here," she said, continuing to cry.

"I'm Platinum Elite, and this is my third day, too!" said a man who obviously was an executive. "My wife here is getting her doctorate in shopping in Milan. Do you know what that is costing me?" said the middle-aged man with a cashmere black blazer, starched white shirt, and pressed khaki pants.

"If you had just gotten us out of here on the first plane instead of messing with Continental, I'd be home where I want to be," said his platinum-haired wife with a new spiky hair cut and obviously a new Milan hair color.

"What do you mean, they can't get you out?" said Mrs. Boyce.

"Look out the window, ma'am," boomed the executive. "Do you see a Continental plane? For some reason, they can't qualify to get in or out of U.S. airspace. They suck! Sorry, girls," he said, looking at Hannah and Niki. "But these are tough times! They keep saying tomorrow, tomorrow, but this is my third tomorrow. And now this plane isn't here, so we aren't going out today either."

"Hank, if you don't get me out of here, I don't know what I'll do. I just checked the departure list, and every single plane is canceled," said his wife returning from checking the departure board.

"Ma'am," said Hank to Mrs. Boyce, who had her cell phone to her ear, "Are you on hold there to Continental? What is it now, 110-minute hold time again? Do you know what that is going to cost you for them to tell you that there are no planes today?"

Mrs. Boyce flipped the cell phone shut and did a fast calculation on how much she'd probably spent already getting that very information. She didn't mind spending money, but she wanted to get some value back. She was glad that she brought the platinum credit card with the huge limit with her. Obviously she was going to need it. "What airlines are flying out?" she said out loud.

"I'll be damned if I know!" said a man in line wearing a yellow Ralph Lauren Polo shirt, blue blazer, and pressed jeans. "I have three sets of tickets, United, American, and Continental. See them?" he said, fanning them out in his hands for everyone in line to see. "I spent ten grand on these tickets right here, and I'm not out of this *city* yet, never mind off this continent. Do you know how many terrorists are right here in Milan? Terrorists even blew a hole in the Uffizi in Florence a few years ago! We are obvious targets, all grouped here in an airport, nice and convenient for a big bomb to hit!"

"Grandma, I'm going to the ladies' room," said Hannah as she darted over to the ladies' bathrooms. She had a take a breath from all this bad news.

"Take your carry-on with you, Hannah," said Mrs. Boyce. "We don't want these guards to detonate it."

As she sat in the stall, Hannah put her head in her hands and allowed herself to cry just a little. She didn't care what else there was to see in Italy. She just wanted to get back on U.S. soil. How were they going to get home if Platinum Man wasn't home yet? Hannah took out her diary and wrote as she sat there.

Dear Diary,

I am so glad that I am here with Grandma and not my cheap mother. Grandma will buy us out of here. We need your help. We can't do this ourselves. Thank you, Lord. Help me to help us in some way. Help us, God.

Love, H

Hannah's writing was interrupted by loud voices just outside her stall.

"We have tickets! We have tickets! Sarah, are you in here?" a woman shouted as she entered the ladies room.

"Yes! I'm in here! How did we get them?" replied Sarah from her stall.

"Your father got them! It was an Oscar-winning performance! He said he would die without his medication, and the ticket agent coughed up tickets on KLM! We leave in an hour! I'm so excited!" she yelled entering a stall and crying profusely.

"How do we know we'll get out this time?" demanded Sarah flushing the toilet. "We have all those tickets Daddy bought, and we're still here!"

"KLM is the only airline really flying out of here! Remember those people we met yesterday? They called us last night to tell us that they got out on KLM! They got to Amsterdam and then caught another plane home."

Hannah quickly dried her eyes and snapped the diary shut.

Mrs. Boyce was up at the ticket counter when Hannah returned. The Continental ticket agent had finally shown up.

"Three weeks from now?" protested Mrs. Boyce. "Where are we supposed to stay until then? The four-hundred-fifty-dollar room we had last night is six hundred fifty dollars tonight! Who knows what it will be tomorrow? I need to get these girls home! When will you get your first plane into this country?"

"Tomorrow" said the agent with an impatient sigh.

"Tomorrow? That is what they told us yesterday! Thanks, anyway," said Mrs. Boyce as she took the new tickets and turned to leave.

Platinum Man came up behind them. "Did you get new tickets? Three weeks from today, right? So did everyone that was here. What's that, a couple hundred people? What about the people who already had tickets for that flight? Man, am I going to do something when I get home!"

"I wish you the best, sir. Girls, let's go over to the main ticket counter and get in line," said Mrs. Boyce.

The three travelers snaked their way through the thousands of people who continued to cram into the airport. Kids screaming, dogs barking in their cages, and disappointed people crying were lying on the floor, sitting on the floor with their backs against walls, or standing in endless lines that wrapped around the terminal.

"Girls, first we are all going to hold hands and pray to be directed to the airline that is really flying out of here. I will give two hundred dollars to St. Anthony if we get tickets that get us to the North American continent. You girls offer to work twenty hours for a charity when we get the tickets. Keep looking out the windows here. See which airline flies in or out. I will stand in line and keep my ears open."

"Grandma, I heard this lady say that KLM is flying out. But you have to go through Amsterdam." Hannah told the story about the lady in the bathroom.

"Wonderful, the Sodom and Gomorrah of Europe. Well, they may have a way to get out, then. Sometimes, there is honor among thieves," said Mrs. Boyce. "Good work, Hannah. God is directing us, and we have to keep our ears open. Niki, why don't you go to the front of the line and listen to who gets tickets to where so we can be prepared when we get up there."

Niki walked up to the front of the line and stood there listening for about a half-hour.

"Mrs. Boyce, they are selling tickets to Vancouver, Canada. I was there with Mom this spring! From Canada, maybe we could fly on the same seaplane Mom and I flew back into Seattle on, or, if we had to, we could drive down from Seattle! It's still a long way from home, but at least we'd be on American soil."

"Excellent work," said Mrs. Boyce, giving Niki a hug. Hannah and Niki high-fived each other.

Two hours later, they got to the front of the line.

The girls crowded up to the counter. Niki sized up the ticket agent—young, maybe competent. More money may work.

"We'd like tickets to California as fast as possible."

"October 6 is the next available flight," said the woman with an indifferent shrug.

"What about first class?" said Mrs. Boyce.

The woman perked up. "Tuesday," she said, typing about a hundred keystrokes quickly.

"What the heck are all those keystrokes?" whispered Hannah to Niki. "When was the last time you typed that much searching for something in a database? What kind of software is this? Circa 1970? Real confidence builder."

"We must get out today," said Mrs. Boyce. "First class and out today, as soon as possible."

Hannah and Niki rolled their eyes at each other. Like they were really going to get out today.

"Is impossible," replied the agent.

"How about a flight from here to Amsterdam and then to Vancouver on KLM today?" countered Mrs. Boyce.

"What about your current tickets?" asked the agent with fake concern.

"I will worry about that later," said Mrs. Boyce. "I understand that I am walking away from those tickets. Please check availability on KLM for today. We are willing to go through Amsterdam and on to Vancouver, Canada."

Hannah, Niki, and Mrs. Boyce stared at the agent who held their future in their hands.

Just then an Italian soldier leaped up onto the ticket counter. The entire crowd stopped talking as the soldier pretended to spray the crowd with bullets from his machine gun. He sneered at the crowd and shouted something in Italian. Some people ducked and others fell to the floor with their hands over their head. Hannah, Niki, and Mrs. Boyce stood firm at the counter, protecting their hard-won position in line.

Niki leaned over. "Is he a cop, or is he a terrorist?"

"I'm not sure," replied Hannah in a whisper. "It is not a good sign that he's pointing a machine gun at us!"

"Get down!" said Mrs. Boyce.

The three of them fell to the floor, crouching behind their carry-on luggage but still pressed against the ticket counter.

Suddenly an older soldier pushed through the crowd on the floor and yelled something in Italian at the soldier on the counter.

Everyone held their breath as they waited to see what would happen next.

Hannah looked up at the counter while pretending to close her eyes.

The soldier on the counter caught the eye of someone on the ground and reluctantly hopped back onto the floor, still sneering at the crowd. His attitude seemed to say, "Okay, not now, but soon."

The older soldier poked him in the back with his gun and pushed him down the stairs and out of the terminal.

Everyone got back up and started talking excitedly at once.

"Oh, my God, that was close!" yelled a girl who bumped into Hannah as she got up. "I can't wait to get out of here! I've never been this scared in my life!" The blue-eyed girl pulled her wild red hair back into a pony tail, wrapping the band over and over it nervously.

"You'll be okay, Kathy" said her forty-something father, putting his arm around her. "This is just temporary. We're not buying new tickets and getting ripped off."

"That's what you think," replied his wife, stumbling to her feet. "No matter what it costs, we're getting out of here today if possible."

Kathy touched Hannah's shoulder. "It is so great to finally see someone my own age! These two have been driving me nuts!"

"I'm Hannah, and this is Niki. I want to get out today, too," agreed Hannah.

"Me too!" said Niki.

"Excuse me miss," said Mrs. Boyce to Kathy. "Girls, please turn to the counter and pay attention," said Mrs. Boyce, worriedly putting her blue pump back on. Hannah and Niki squeezed hands and looked back at the ticket agent. The agent continued to type without pause.

"I may have something," the agent said to Mrs. Boyce, Hannah, and Niki. "A new flight is being put together for Americans. It goes to Amsterdam, and then another flight leaves for Vancouver at five this afternoon. I have three first-class tickets left. Do you want them?" she asked them.

"Yes," said Mrs. Boyce, instinctively knowing not to ask about the price.

With a quick swipe of the platinum credit card, the tickets spat out of the machine. Mrs. Boyce, Niki, and Hannah all burst out crying with relief as Mrs. Boyce clutched the tickets in her hand.

Kathy's parents stepped up out of the line and questioned them. "Are you getting out?" one woman asked.

"Yes, for two thousand dollars each to Amsterdam and on to Vancouver," said Mrs. Boyce, not wishing to mislead anyone. "And we're not out yet. We only have tickets. God bless you. Let's go, girls."

"I'm not paying that!" said Kathy's father.

"You are too! Are there any other flights out?" her mother asked, gripping the counter as Mrs. Boyce, Hannah, and Niki wheeled their carry-ons to get to the gate.

"Thank God we are not with her father," thought Hannah.

They descended into the duty-free area reserved for lucky people with tickets for scheduled flights. They looked for their flight on the monitor.

"It's not there!" said Hannah.

"No, it's not," replied Mrs. Boyce. "Let's go, girls. I believe that agent is putting the flight together, and for some reason we were lucky enough to get on it. We are clearly on faith, but just getting down here is good. Thank you, Lord and St. Anthony. So far, so good. Girls, spend the rest of your lira except for souvenir cash, and meet me at counter number 40. I'm going to get the *New York Times* and some other decent reading materials to see what is really going on in the United States."

Hannah decided on a watch for her sister, Christine.

"What a nice watch," said Tony, suddenly right behind her. "I guess you didn't find a watch when you were searching my office the other night, and now you must purchase one before you leave?" he asked with a neutral tone.

"Hi, Tony, what are you doing here? It was really nice of you to get us those tickets to Milan. We might actually get back to North America tonight!" said Niki coolly, ignoring the reference to their sojourn of the other night. It seemed so long ago. There must have been cameras, she surmised.

"I have a business trip, Niki. Hannah, I see you have your laptop. That is good. I am going to Amsterdam and Vancouver on that secret American getaway flight! I have to admit, you Americans are resourceful. Of course, with those terrorist cells planted over there already, maybe you should stay here! I would be happy to escort you to the places that you have missed until things quiet down," he said with a wink to the girls.

"How are you getting on the American flight, Tony?" probed Hannah. "Can't you postpone your trip? It's scary to fly now!"

"I have some winery connections. It is not to worry. I will protect you on the flight," he said over his shoulder while walking away.

"What's he doing here?" asked Niki as they watched him leave.

"Girls, let's go," said Mrs. Boyce nervously walking up to them. "I asked you to meet me. The plane is boarding. Let's not miss it!"

"Sorry! Sorry!" they yelled, quickly paying for their purchases and following Mrs. Boyce to the gate.

Just at the gate, Kathy ran up to them "We got tickets too! My flight number is 492. What is your flight number? Here is my email address. Email me when you land safely. What is your email address and I'll email you!"

"Hannah@secondrisingranch.com," said Hannah. "Email us too!"

Mrs. Boyce smiled approval. That was the address that she gave anyone she didn't know very well.

"Miss, your ticket," said the agent to Hannah firmly.

Hannah and Niki gave thumbs-up to Kathy and hurried down toward the plane

Soon they were settled on the plane in first class. When the plane lifted off, everyone clapped and cheered. Some people were crying with relief. In two short hours, they landed in the clean and modern Amsterdam airport. The girls were cautiously jubilant.

"McDonalds! Burger King! It's clean! No jerks on counters with machine guns! Hurray! Hurray!" shouted Hannah, giving her grandmother a hug. "Let's log on and update everyone on our progress!"

"Okay, girls, we'll go to the first-class lounge for KLM. You can plug in that laptop and re-charge it again, just in case," said Mrs. Boyce.

"We won't need it again, Grandma," protested Hannah. "We're back in civilization!"

"Hannah, please plug the laptop in near where I sit in the lounge, and you can go use the club PCs. We are not home yet."

"Okay, Grandma," said Hannah, not wanting to drag the laptop out again.

Just as Hannah sent her last email, they all heard an announcement. "We are boarding flight 123 to Vancouver early. All passengers proceed to the gate."

"Are we in the *X-Files*? These outfits are really retro!" Hannah said when they arrived at the gate. Women in red/orange suits and high heels were taking tickets. The name on the plane read "Trumpet Airlines."

As they settled into their seats, Tony stopped by. "Oh, first class. I should have known!" he said to the girls while Mrs. Boyce was loading her carry-on above her seat. "Of course. That is where all the action is now!" he said and crisply walked over to his own first-class bulkhead seat directly behind the cockpit door."

Hannah swiped her index finger across her throat as she turned to Niki. "Great. Right near us!" said Hannah to Niki in a low voice.

"Take out your laptop as soon as we get up in the air," whispered Niki. "If he heads for the cockpit door you can throw it at him, and I will rush up there."

"Okay," agreed Hannah. "I'll go and get some blankets, too. If we crash, they will absorb the plane fuel, and we'll have a better chance of escape."

Little did the teens know that this would be a plane ride they would never forget.

Chapter 10
Plane Ride

$\mathcal{M}$rs. Boyce was seated next to a handsome senior in the last row of the first-class cabin, and Hannah and Niki were seated in the second row in the two center seats. At first both girls were skeptical that their center aisle seats were going to be a good thing. But once the flight got underway, they soon realized the advantage of both having aisle seats. The man in the seat across the aisle immediately fell asleep, leaving the man next to the window stranded and stuck. That man eventually shed his shoes and literally leaped over the sleeping passenger to get to the restroom.

"I wonder what the movie is going to be," Niki said as she started to rummage through the seat pocket in front of her. She pulled out a very strange emergency instruction sheet. The characters in the illustrations looked more like munchkins than actual flight attendants.

"Let's just hope there is more than one feature film," Hannah added. "This is a twelve hour or more flight."

"Oh, no!" Niki wailed. "Look at this. *Dr. Doolittle II*!" Again!

"No way! Let me see that!" Hannah demanded as she yanked the photocopied food menu and film list right out of Niki's hands.

Acting stunned, Niki turned to Hannah. "I can't believe that we're going to be subjected to that talk-with-the-animals drivel one more time. And what is up with the cheap list instead of a real in-flight magazine?" Then she stuck her index finger into her mouth and made a gagging noise.

Hannah and Niki both laughed, probably just a little too loudly.

"Keep it down up there, you two." Hannah could hear her grandmother's voice from way in the back.

"Sorry, Grandma." Hannah turned around and smiled at her lovely grandmother.

"Kiss-up," Niki chided.

"Dumb blond," Hannah retorted.

"Let's get this show on the road." Niki fidgeted in her seat.

"No kidding. Let's go," Hannah added, looking over both of her shoulders before settling into her seat.

"Niki. Look over there," Hannah said, pointing to the split in the curtain between the tiny first-class section and the first row of the coach cabin. "There's a girl crying her eyes out back there. I wonder what's wrong?" said Hannah.

Just then the pilot interrupted the Muzac with his first announcement. "Ladies and gentlemen," he greeted his passengers with perfect diction and a Dutch accent. "There seems to be some problem with the closing mechanism on the door, and before we lift off we will be inspecting the bottom of the plane for any bombs."

Hannah froze in her seat. Her immediate fear temporarily struck her speechless.

Niki's attention was elsewhere while the announcement was being made, and she really didn't register what the pilot had said. "I'm going to have a walk around the plane. My legs are getting stiff," Niki said, and, without waiting for an acknowledgment from Hannah, she unbelted her seat belt and stood up.

Hannah was temporarily stricken with terror. She grabbed her diary and wrote quickly.

Dear Diary,

What if they blow up the plane? What if we are stuck in Amsterdam and can't get home for years? Am I having a panic attack? I am going to breathe.

Bye Bye,

H

Hannah began to pace herself through the breathing exercises she learned in yoga class.

Niki strolled down the first-class section and poked her head through to the coach section. Looking down, Niki's eyes met the swollen red eyes of the girl sitting in the first row of coach.

"I'm sorry," Niki said to her. "I don't mean to intrude or anything. Is anyone sitting there? Niki nodded toward the empty seat next to the sad young girl.

"Yes, but he seems to be wandering around somewhere. He's an exchange student and doesn't speak much English."

"Another one of those on student visas, huh?" Niki asked.

"Yes, he's from Milan and studies at Yale or Boston College. I'm not really sure. Oh, my name is Nancy Shellerman."

"Niki Parker," Niki nodded. "Is there anything I can do for you? You seem upset."

"I am upset. My dad has been reported among the missing in the World Trade Center. I just don't believe it. Mom is in South China working on a fossil find, and my brother is returning from his tour on the *USS Ben Franklin*. He's been stationed God-knows-where for the last five months, and he's due to be home any day now. Or at least that was the plan before all of this mess." Nancy started to cry again.

"I know that there are Web sites with lists of the people believed to be missing, but since I left the university in Milan I haven't had any access to the Internet," Nancy added.

"Once we get underway, I think we'll be able to get online with my friend Hannah's laptop. It's equipped with a satellite uplink, and boy has it come in handy," Niki said as she looked at Nancy reassuringly.

"I'd appreciate it if you'd have a chance to look for any information about him. His name is Kevin Shellerman. He worked for Roncatell, Inc."

"No problem." Niki stood up to leave as the foreign-exchange student approached his seat. "Don't worry, Nancy. If there's any news at all, we'll let you know."

Niki started toward her seat but had a change of mind. She decided to have a look at the entire plane.

As Niki entered the first-class cabin, she saw that Tony had his laptop open and looked like he was logging on to a Web site. Slowing her pace, Niki paused behind Tony and took a good look at the URL on the screen as she headed for the bathroom up front.

www.threeheaddragon.com

She memorized his keystrokes as he typed his name and password in the dialog boxes.

```
Tony

3dragons
```

"There is that three dragons again," Niki thought as she quickly returned to her seat next to Hannah.

Sitting down, Niki could hardly control herself. "I have important things to tell you, but first I have to write something down," Niki said, grabbing a pen and the in-flight magazine to jot down the URL and the name and password she'd observed. "Tony had this on his laptop. I memorized the URL, his login, and his password as he typed it." Niki motioned toward Tony, who was apparently having computer problems. He seemed to be slamming the Ctrl/Alt/Del keys over and over again.

"Let me type it in."

Hannah closed out her email and Niki typed in the address and password.

```
"Web Page Not Available"
displayed on the screen.
```

"Bookmark the Web address anyway, Niki. We better shut down. Here comes the shopping cart," said Hannah.

"Okay. I introduced myself to a girl who's crying back there in coach," Niki raced on. "Her name is Nancy Shellerman, and her father is on the WTC missing list. She hasn't had any word from her family since she left the dorm at the university in Milan where she is a student. And she's doesn't have a phone. I told her that we'd log on to the World Trade Center Web sites and let her know if there's any news about her dad." Niki typed in the URL and then looked for Nancy's father's name. "There it is," said Niki. "He is still listed as missing. I feel so sorry for her."

"That stinks," said Hannah. "Good work though getting Tony's password, Ms. Tracy," said Hannah as she tried to stifle her mounting fear as she observed men scurrying around just outside the plane. "Why didn't they take off? Did they find something?"

Just then the duty-free cart stopped at the girls' seat. It had alcoholic beverages, sodas, water, and the cutest dolls dressed in the bright orange Trumpet Air flight attendant's uniform. "I have to have one of those dolls; no one will believe these outfits," said Niki. "Do you want one, too, Hannah?"

"Sure do. We'll have two of those dolls, please." Hannah handed the attendant her grandmother's credit card. "Perhaps I'd better ask first." Hannah dashed down the aisle to talk to her grandmother.

Niki stuffed one of the dolls into her carry-on bag and promptly forgot about it.

"Grandma says okay," Hannah said to the attendant, took the credit card receipt, and stuffed her doll into her carry-on bag. "This is cool. Proof that Trumpet Air has outfits from the way future or past."

Just then the captain's voice boomed over the speaker: "Everyone to their seats! Buckle up, in-flight attendants. We're the last flight out if we leave in the next five minutes. Close every overhead now! Shut down the cell phones, and sit down. I can't take off if even one of you is not sitting."

Everyone scrambled to their seats, and anyone not sitting or messing around with the overhead was threatened immediately by seated passengers.

Soon they ascended into the air. Hannah exhaled deeply and felt a tear of relief roll down her cheek.

As soon as the plane stabilized, they served weird-looking Jell-O stuff with pieces of partially cooked fish embedded in it.

"This is disgusting!" Hannah whispered to Niki.

Hannah hid the mystery fish stuff under the droopy leaf of lettuce she suspected was supposed to become part of a weird fish sandwich. The slice of cheese looked pretty normal, but it didn't taste normal. And the little roll was so hard Niki had to dunk it into her salad dressing to make it chewable.

"I hope we get another meal down the road some. This is not going to hold me. Oh, what I'd give for another hamburger and French fries," Hannah lamented.

"A chocolate milkshake and tuna sandwich sounds good to me," Niki added. "Let's not talk about food." Both girls nodded in agreement.

And then, *Doctor Doolittle II* began on the in-flight entertainment TV. Only this time it was dubbed into Dutch.

Next, the passenger parade to the bathroom began. After each passenger went into the first-class section's restroom, either Hannah or Niki got up and went to the bathroom to check for suspicious packages.

"I have no idea what we are looking for, but I just have a hunch that something is about to turn up. I just don't want to miss it," Hannah said to Niki, poking her and reminding her that it was her turn to check out the restroom after Tony left the lavatory.

"Hmmm. Nothing here to speak of," Niki said to herself as she washed her hands before she opened the door. As she opened the door she was immediately confronted with the flight attendant who was looking at her intently. "Is there anything I can do for you, miss?" the attendant asked Niki.

"Oh, no. I'm fine. Just have a tiny bladder, that's all." Niki blushed pushing past her in the tiny aisle.

As Niki hurried back to her seat, Tony practically knocked her down as he pushed past her and bolted into the bathroom again.

If the attendant hadn't been standing right there, Niki would have put her ear to the door, but, then again, that would have been really tacky.

Niki hurried back to her seat. "Did you see who just went in there again?" Niki asked Hannah.

"Tony!" Hannah said excitedly. "What the heck is he doing in there again?"

"Maybe he has a tiny bladder, too," laughed Niki.

As Tony left the bathroom, Hannah dashed up the other aisle and cut in front of the flight attendant, who was only two steps away and heading in that direction.

Hannah flipped the door lock shut, and her eyes quickly adjusted to the increased illumination. "This is the fourth time I've washed my hands," she noted mentally as she attended to the task. She dropped the paper towel as she tried to shove it into the overflowing trash slot. She felt guilty for a minute, realizing that she and Niki had probably contributed to the overflow with their many trips to the bathroom.

"Now, what's that?" Hannah said out loud, bending down in the cramped space to get a better look at what was wedged in the crack in the flooring. Hannah touched the object with her fingertip. Picking it up she gently lifted it to take a closer look. "Well, what a coincidence," Hannah again spoke right out loud.

Tucking the little object safely into her jacket, Hannah hurried back to her seat, but who was standing there but Tony, as big as life, talking to Niki.

"Do you happen to have a traveler's sewing kit by any chance?" Tony was asking Niki in his most continental way.

"I think I do," Niki said digging around in her carry-on, readjusting the contents, and situating her new doll at the bottom of the bag. "Here it is," Niki said, handing the little plastic box over to Tony. "He either looked like a total hunk or the perfect devil," Hannah reflected briefly.

"Thank you. I will return it after I sew up my shirt sleeve." Tony smiled as if asking Niki to sew it up for him.

"Can I sew that up for you?" Hannah offered before Niki could speak.

"Oh, no. I'll do it myself. I couldn't impose." Tony slipped back to his seat, sewing kit in hand.

"What's with the Martha-Stewart act, Hannah? When was the last time you sewed anything?" asked Niki with mock horror.

"Niki, over here. Look what I found." Hannah carefully handed Niki the item she found on the floor.

"Cool, Hannah? You've found a broken three-headed dragon cufflink with diamond-studded eyes. What is it with the three-headed dragon? In the Duomo, Tony said it fought the enemies of God," whispered Hannah. "I'm wondering if the United States is an enemy of God in his opinion."

Bam. The plane hit a sudden patch of turbulence, and Niki and Hannah both decided to buckle up.

Bam—more turbulence. Hannah looked over at Niki, her eyes wide with fear. Niki grabbed Hannah's hand.

"What is it?" asked Niki. "Please let it be turbulence."

"At least Tony is still in his seat," said Hannah.

Hannah tabbed over to the news web site. "Oh, my God! What is Kathy's flight number?"

"492," replied Niki immediately looking over at the laptop. "Why?"

"Oh, my God! 492—Kathy's flight crashed in Milan on takeoff! And look! There's a three-headed dragon on the bottom of the screen on the news story, right on the laptop screen!

Niki grabbed Hannah's hand again. "Oh, no!" They both looked up at Tony at the same time.

Just at that second, Tony looked back at them and laughed. He turned back to the front of the plane, closed his laptop gently, and ran his hands over the cover.

"Are we going to crash? Is he a suicide hijacker? If he is involved, we have to try and stop him," said Niki with determination.

"We have to think of a plan!" replied Hannah.

The pilot's voice crackled over the intercom with another announcement. "Ladies and gentlemen. I am sorry to inform you that there have been threats of additional international terrorism directed at symbols of American capitalism. All aircraft in this airspace have been diverted for immediate grounding. We have been diverted to Reykjavik, Iceland."

"I can't believe it!" said Hannah as another tear rolled down her cheek. "We were on our way! We were going to be in Canada tonight. This is so wrong!" she cried.

"I hope we're not being hijacked," whispered Niki, crying, too.

Niki and Hannah both looked at each other and wiped the tears away. It was time to get to work.

"Let's get out the laptop again and check that URL I got from Tony now," said Niki.

Niki entered the URL and the username and password she'd written down on the magazine and pressed Enter.

The login took longer than seemed necessary but finally the screen opened. It was an image of a three-headed dragon. The picture had a funny grainy quality to it. Hannah saved it; it took a long time to download. She attached the picture to an email that told Aunt Mel they were being diverted, and sent it to Aunt Mel. Just as she pressed Send, Hannah got a warning that the battery was running low and it was time to shut down.

"Did it go through?" asked Niki when they didn't get a confirmation dialog box.

"I don't know. At least we got the picture," Hannah said. "We'll need electricity before we can have a closer look at that picture and resend that email. I just know it's important. Could it be three guys that represent the three heads? Is Tony one of them? Unless they've developed a new enemy, I think we have to assume it could be us. Maybe he is trying to use us for something."

"What could it be? Great job getting that picture, Hannah. He keeps asking about your laptop. He has a laptop. What makes yours so different? Is it the satellite uplink?" replied Niki.

"I know it's something important, too, but there's nothing we can do about it right now. It's almost time to land in that sunny paradise known as Iceland,." replied Hannah.

Just before they landed, Tony stepped up, leaned over, and spoke softly to Hannah. "Did you hear about that unfortunate crash in Milan? I wonder if your new friend Kathy made it? Glad to see you made it out with that laptop," said Tony. "It would have been a shame to lose that icon of American technology. I'll see you in Iceland," he said as he walked back to his seat.

"He is evil. What is he up to? Please let him just sit down and not head for the cockpit," said Niki to Hannah. They both let out a huge sigh of relief when Tony buckled himself back in his seat.

Chapter 11
Diverted!

"**I**'ve been to this frigid hole in the wall with my dad on a fish research assignment," said Hannah as the plane banked to the left toward Iceland. "We stayed up at Saint Michael's College during spring break. Even then, it was two to five degrees every day and much colder out on the water with the fish with those other marine biologists. I hope they put us up at the college. I think that is the only place on the island for this many people—unless they stick us in a gym somewhere," said Hannah.

"I hope if we land safely that they let us off the plane," said Niki. "You know they made people on the other flights stay on the planes for thirty hours after the terrorists bombed the twin towers. They just got out yesterday! I wonder what the problem is. I hope it is not our friend Tony."

"Let's go over to my grandmother's seat and see what she thinks is happening before we land," said Hannah. The older gentleman next to her went up to the bathroom as they arrived. As they plopped down, Grandma was enjoying a hot cup of tea.

"Grandma, that girl Kathy's plane crashed in Milan! I hope we don't crash. I hope we stay at St. Michael's. It's nice, and I was there with Daddy. You don't think we're being hijacked, do you? What do you think Tony is up to? Did he steal the diamonds? Is he is fencing them for someone?" rambled Hannah. She couldn't help herself.

"I don't know what to think about Tony and his diamonds," replied Mrs. Boyce.

Hannah raced on. "Enrico told us that the Florence investigators believe that a cell of terrorists in Italy are buying precious gems like diamonds, smuggling them into the U.S., fencing them, and then using the money to fund terror attacks!" said Hannah in a rush, where she lost her breath at the end.

"That poor girl and her parents. I pray that they are okay. No matter what you call it, we think that Tony may have a lot of diamonds with him," said Mrs. Boyce. "It is either an unholy coincidence, or he is up to no good. Look at this article in the *National Geographic* I picked up in Milan. I just got a chance to read it. It says that diamonds are used by terrorists to fund acts of terror. In all fairness, Tony was nice to us in Florence. We have no proof. He being a terrorist sounds outrageous, but we don't know whom we can trust here. Let's say a quick prayer that God will lead us to the right people and show us what to do if we encounter a problem. We need to get an email to Mel and ask her to look into Tony."

"I tried to send her an email but my laptop battery is dead. I don't know if it went through."

"We need to tell her to look up three-headed dragons, too! It keeps popping up: it was in Tony's office; he has three-headed dragon cufflinks; he even dropped one in the bathroom. I have it right here!" said Hannah, showing Mrs. Boyce the cufflink.

"What?" said Mrs. Boyce.

"And Mrs. Boyce! We did see Tony buying the diamonds, and he is from the Middle East," countered Niki. "I don't want to be prejudiced, but I'm scared!"

"Eduardo was very suspicious about Tony, too," said Mrs. Boyce. "If he is smuggling diamonds into the country, his timing could not be worse, with his ethnicity. Please come over and stand by me as we deplane. We are beginning the descent. Let's all say a prayer and then you go back to your seats."

Soon the plane bumped to a landing.

"Thank you, God," said Hannah. "I wonder what is next?"

The passengers emptied out of the plane onto the tarmac and were led to the waiting room. The rumor about the plane crash in Milan spread like wildfire. Everyone was afraid.

A pert twenty-something girl with red hair cut short and flipped out stepped up to the microphone at the ticket counter to speak. She tapped the microphone.

"Welcome to Reykjavik. We wish it were different circumstances. We've housed the other people stranded here since the tragedy, and they went home yesterday. I am your Red Cross representative, and my name is Maureen."

"Saint Michael's College has not started fall school term, and the cleaning people just finished cleaning there. So that is where you will be staying tonight. It's quite lovely. Married couples can stay in married student housing, and the rest will be divided into the women's and men's dorms by gender."

Hannah walked up to Maureen quickly. "Can we stay in the Marian girls' dorm?" Hannah asked her. "I've stayed here with my dad on a marine-biology project. In the resident advisor's suite? This is my grandmother, Mrs. Boyce, and my friend, Niki, and we'd all like to stay together. And I know the resident advisor's suite has two bedrooms."

"Sure, nice to meet you all," said Maureen. "Room 202, right down the first-floor hall of the girls' dorm. Hop on bus number three. Here are your keys. I am so sorry that you folks have to go through this. We are not sure of the cause, but we will do everything we can to make your stay pleasant. You'll be served dinner in the college cafeteria." Maureen turned to a Midwestern couple. "How can I help?"

"Great!" said Hannah. "That room rocks! I visited it when I was here. It even has a place to recharge my laptop, and we can connect to the Internet with a land line and look at that picture again."

"Well, can you share your laptop with me?" asked Tony coming up behind them.

"No men allowed in the girls' dorm. Sorry, sir," said Maureen sternly.

Hannah winced at Niki when she realized that Tony overheard her. She had to start keeping her big mouth shut.

The yellow school bus bumped up the road to the St. Michael's girls' dorm. The dorm rose up in front of them, a huge Tudor mansion with a three-story round turret room and ivy climbing up the walls.

"It looks old, but it has been renovated inside," said Hannah. "I love the turret. It reminds me of my room at your place, Grandma."

More volunteers welcomed them, and the three hurried to the resident advisor's room with Hannah in the lead. The college advisor's suite was the first floor of the turret. They stepped into a round living space split into sections. One section was a small kitchen; next to it on the wall was a workstation area with plugs and setup for laptops; and then a bedroom off each side of the living room. Oversized chairs and couches were in the middle of the room.

"This does rock!" said Niki. "Let's set up the computer."

"Girls, email Mel, and tell her what we know, ASAP," said Mrs. Boyce. "Then email your parents, and tell them where we are. Send an email to that girl, Kathy, too. Just because the plane crashed does not mean that she is dead. The Red Cross volunteer, Maureen, said that we're leaving tomorrow morning. The reason that we are here is that an international flight had a deranged passenger on a plane from London to Boston, so they diverted all flights flying into the U.S. It does not appear to be terrorist-related. Remind your parents that we are flying into Vancouver. We'll try to fly back into the United States, but, worst case, we are driving back on Monday into the United States and going to my house in Calistoga. They can pick you up there when they can get back to the West Coast.

"I'm going to take a nap before dinner," continued Grandma. "Do not leave the building and try not to get on TV this time. It may be a long night, and I'm feeling my years right now. Good job on getting us this palatial suite, Hannah. I am grateful to have a clean bed."

"Okay. We'll wake you up if anything big happens this time, Grandma, I promise," said Hannah. She plugged the laptop into the wall using her electricity adapter.

"Here we are," Hannah said as the laptop booted. "It's great to see that battery start to charge! I downloaded the dragon picture here."

"What the heck does the three-headed dragon mean in 2001? Is Tony really part of a jihad? Why would a rich guy like that want to be a terrorist? I don't get it. Why don't people like that want to use their talents for good instead of killing other people, and themselves too!" asked Niki. "Let me play around with the file. Do you have Adobe Illustrator on this?"

"Yeah, double-click the face icon on the desktop," said Hannah. "The Irish killed each other for years in Northern Ireland."

"Hmm, nothing," said Niki opening the file. "I'm going to search the news for anything on pictures. It's hard to know how to search for it."

"Go to the msnbc.com site," said Hannah.

"Look. Oh, my gosh!" Niki clicked and clicked again. "This could be it! It says here that some terrorists are hiding messages in picture jpegs! I bet Tony *is* a terrorist!"

"Okay. Does it say how to get the message out of the picture file?" asked Hannah.

Niki played around with the picture jpeg again. "Here is a text message!" said Niki as she pointed to the screen. I just selected the text box and changed the text color to white! Now you can see it against the dark background."

"Bring the diamonds to Jersey City 3 PM Tuesday."

Niki's hands were shaking.

"Email it to Mel quick!" said Hannah. "Now, let's search on Tony, find a picture of him, and send it to Mel. How about searching the Florence newspapers. Search on 'wine.' I bet he had his mug on the social page."

"Here it is!" said Niki, displaying the Florence newspaper's society page online showing Tony shaking hands at the wine show with Mrs. Boyce. "Oh, no!" said Niki. "It's the one they took of him shaking hands with your grandmother! I hope this isn't the shot that they distributed all over the flipping world."

"Great. I don't want Grandma hurt. But Mel won't hurt my grandmother. Send it to Mel!" said Hannah looking over Niki's shoulder at the laptop screen. "Hurry!"

Niki attached the picture to an email and quickly pressed Send. "I hope he isn't a terrorist. Your grandmother will be questioned and maybe hounded by the tabloids. You've seen what they do to my mother."

"Hopefully your investigative-reporter aunt can find out who he is. She has contacts all over the world. I'll connect the printer to the laptop," said Hannah. She sat down and downloaded a driver for the printer, hooked up the cables, rebooted, and printed the picture five times. Soon some of the other female passengers, who happened to be models trying to get back home, started filtering into the room.

"What are you doing?" said one of the passengers. "Can we send emails to people, telling them where we are?"

"Sure," said Hannah, "just let me print this and send one email. Then you can use it."

"Who is that?" said one of the models from Milan, looking at Tony's picture displayed on the monitor.

"We think he could be a terrorist smuggling diamonds into the U.S. to fund more attacks!" said Hannah.

"What? I just saw that guy creeping around the building. Maybe he's after your computer. I think he had problems with his on board," said the model.

"He seems to be very interested in my laptop. Let's leave the laptop here and pretend to go to dinner," suggested Hannah.

"That's good," said Niki. "When he tries to get it, we'll jump him, throw blankets on him, and tie him up!"

"We're going to need help," said Hannah to the group of assorted passengers.

"I'll help!" said one of the models.

"Me, too!" said two of the flight attendants.

"What's going on out here?" asked Mrs. Boyce, coming out of her room fresh from her nap and a shower and surveying the growing crowd in the room.

Quickly the girls filled her in on the plan.

"Normally, I would insist on calling the police, but as long as you emailed Mel, I think we should act as soon as possible. Mel is waiting for our messages. Tony will never suspect that we know anything. Maybe he needs the laptop to fulfill his mission in Jersey City. If he doesn't try to get the laptop, we can just go on to dinner and make the next plan."

"Let's go out the door like we're going to dinner. We'll circle back, and we'll get him when he comes to get the laptop," said Niki. "Some of you will have to stay here."

The models stayed in the room, since their shoes were the least appropriate for running. The flight attendants returned to their rooms down the hall. Still others hid in the bathroom in case he made it down the hall.

Hannah and Niki left the building with Mrs. Boyce. They sneaked back to the room as planned.

"I can't believe we are doing this," said Hannah, grabbing a blanket off the bed. "I can throw this over him."

"Shhh! Shhh!" said some of the girls. Everyone held their collective breath.

"We've got to get him!" said Mrs. Boyce, who hid behind the door with her hair dryer poised as a weapon. Hannah and Niki ducked behind the couch in the common room.

Soon, the doorknob turned and in sneaked Tony. He grabbed the laptop case and started to leave.

"I knew it, you terrorist!" said Niki as she jumped out in front of him.

Hannah ran over and dropped to her knees behind Tony. As planned, Niki ran up and pushed him back over Hannah so that Tony sprawled onto the floor. Hannah rolled over and threw a blanket over him.

Tony struggled under the blanket and grabbed for the laptop case again.

Mrs. Boyce ran out from behind the door and smashed him on the head with the hair dryer. Hannah grabbed the laptop case, and she and Tony began a ferocious tug of war for the case.

"Let it go!" shouted Tony. "I don't want to hurt you!"

Niki grabbed the laptop case strap. As she did, the side of the case ripped and dozens of diamonds bounced all over the dorm-room floor.

"Oh, my God!" said Hannah. "You hid them in my laptop case at the wine show! That's why you've been following us! You don't want the laptop; you hid the diamonds in my laptop case!"

Tony, Hannah, Niki, and Grandma fell onto the diamonds, trying to gather them up.

"Help! Help!" yelled Niki. The female passengers came running from everywhere. Some fell on the diamonds, and the models threw shoes and hair dryers at Tony. Finally all of the girls wrestled him onto the floor.

"Hold him!" shouted Hannah.

"Hurry!" said Niki, holding a kicking leg.

"Hurry," said Grandma, holding an arm.

One of the flight attendants crouched down and hooked her arm around Tony's neck in a choke-hold and pulled hard.

"I knew this would come in handy someday," said the perky flight attendant triumphantly.

Tony gasped for breath. His face filled with rage, and he flailed and kicked to get free.

Hannah grabbed a lamp, ripped off the electric cord, and tied Tony's hands together. Niki grabbed another cord and tied his feet.

All of the girls pushed Tony into a chair and tied him to it with more cords. Soon no lamps in the room had cords.

"Great job, everyone!" said Mrs. Boyce to the happy winners. She hesitantly walked up to Tony. "I bet you were bringing those diamonds to finance future attacks! You are despicable!"

"You bitches! After I helped you get out of Florence," sputtered Tony.

"Bet it just kills you that we 'bitches' caught you," said Hannah emphatically. "The only reason you helped us was to get the diamonds off the European continent! Are you a terrorist? Are you one of the heads on the three-headed dragon? Who are the other two? What are your plans? What did we ever do to you?"

"Do you think I am going to tell you anything?" said Tony. "Haven't you ruined enough?

"You Americans think you are always right! You stash your armies in Saudi Arabia, in defiance of Muslim law, and you support Israel over the Palestinians that were driven from their land. Now you will pay attention to our issues! This is *jihad*! You American women are the worst!"

"Why do you blame Americans for everything that is wrong with your world? Why did you have to bring your violence to our shores? I have never done anything to you," said Mrs. Boyce. "But you and your group participated in killing thousands of Americans in cold blood. You make me sick! Why?" asked Mrs. Boyce again.

"The Palestinians supported you during World War II, and how did you repay them? By giving Israel, Egypt, and Jordan their land! Liars! You make me sick! Death to all of you!" replied Tony. Tony spat at Mrs. Boyce, and it slid down her arm.

Suddenly Mrs. Boyce smacked Tony right in the face.

"You pig!" shouted Hannah, and she rushed over and smacked him really hard.

"How dare you spit at Mrs. Boyce!" said Niki, and she smacked him.

"This is for my missing father! You're not even sorry!" said Nancy, smacking Tony so hard that his head snapped back.

Many of the female passengers raced up and took turns smacking Tony in the face.

By the time the local police arrived to take Tony away, he had two black eyes started and his face was swollen from the slapping.

Sirens rang out, and the girls could see flashing lights as they pulled up to the dorm.

"The police are here!" shouted one of the models.

"They got carried away!" Tony shouted to the police as they rushed into the room. "Brutality!"

The young police officers stopped and leaned up against the wall to balance themselves, because they were laughing so hard.

"Imagine that! Girls catching and beating up a powerful terrorist!" said a big burly policeman as he untied Tony to handcuff him.

"They should be charged!" yelled Tony indignantly.

The blond policeman was laughing so hard that he had to sit down. Mrs. Boyce and the girls laughed, too. It felt like the first time they had laughed since the attack.

"What do we charge them for?" asked the policeman when he finally stopped laughing. "I think I saw you slip on a banana peel and get those injuries, didn't he, folks? We've got you! Better than your fellow chicken terrorists who killed innocent people and then died so we can't get them. But you'll get to pay for all of their sins, too!" he continued while handcuffing Tony who was still struggling.

"Look at these diamonds!" said Hannah, stepping forward with the diamonds collected in a drawer that they had pulled out of a desk.

"We decoded a message telling him to bring them to Jersey City on Tuesday!" said Hannah.

"That would be to hand them off to your fence there, isn't that right, Tony?" said a swarthy man stepping up from the background.

"Who are you?" asked Mrs. Boyce suspicious.

"Well you must be Mrs. Boyce. Glad to meet you. I'm Frank McCauly," said the man. "Mel called me after she got your email, and I called the local police. She's been researching the diamond part of the story since you girls reported Tony here buying the diamonds with that girl. I was on assignment with Mel in Desert Storm! I've been here covering the 9/11 diverted flights story."

"Thank you," said Mrs. Boyce, straightening her hair as she reached out to shake his hand.

"I can see that you didn't need us! You caught this guy all by yourselves!"

Tony spat in the direction of Hannah and Niki. "You were following me! If it wasn't for me, you'd still be stuck in Florence!"

"Actually, we weren't following you," said Niki. "We were in the alley waiting for Mrs. Boyce. What about your friends who murdered the innocent Americans?"

"Innocent! Americans? I don't think so! Your army shot missiles right into my village after the African embassies were attacked!" yelled Tony. "You killed my mother and my sister! You occupy sacred land! You'll see! We are everywhere! We will win!" shouted Tony with his eyes swelling shut as he was placed into the police car.

"You didn't win today, thank God," said Mrs. Boyce from the steps to the dorm as the police loaded Tony into the police car.

"I think it's time for celebration!" said Maureen, the Red Cross volunteer, running up the walkway to the dorm. "Let's go to dinner!"

The plane passengers ate heartily and sang American folk songs with local musicians long into the night. There were a lot of hugs as the passengers left the cafeteria to return to their rooms.

The next day all of the passengers marched back onto the plane for the trip to Vancouver on Trumpet Air.

The three travelers watched the model of a plane as it slowly crossed the continent on the map displayed in the front of the plane. It seemed like it took forever.

When they finally arrived in Vancouver, there was more bad news. Every plane out of Vancouver was canceled. The passengers exchanged addresses and hugged goodbye.

The three rented a hotel room at the airport after renting an SUV to drive home to California.

"Twenty-two hours, Grandma. That's a long drive! If it was two years from now, I could drive, Grandma!" said Hannah as they flopped into bed.

Just as the sun began to rise the next morning, they hopped into the SUV and drove to the border.

"This is scary driving in the dark not knowing what or who is out there," said Mrs. Boyce when they started. They all looked into each car suspiciously.

After waiting an hour at the border, they managed to get across.

"Girls, start calling the airlines in the Seattle airport. See if you can find an open flight to San Jose. With all those people stranded up in Vancouver there must be some open seats!"

Both girls pulled out their American cell phones and began dialing directory assistance and then each airline, one by one.

"Got one," said Hannah, taking her grandmother's credit card to charge them.

They stopped in Seattle and flew home to San Jose on standby. Mel picked them up at the airport and drove them back to Mrs. Boyce's house, since neither of their parents could get to the West Coast to meet them.

The girls raced up to Hannah's room and logged on.

"Niki! Here's an email from Kathy! She and her parents made it! Oh, thank God!" she said, happily hitting reply.

"Email her right back!" said Niki emphatically.

After emailing all of their friends, Niki pulled out her Trumpet Air doll from her carry-on and said, "Let's find Trumpet Air," said Niki.

Hannah got her Trumpet Air doll from her carry-on, and they sat them side by side on the side of the phone table.

They typed in the URL listed on the Trumpet Airlines dolls' bags. "Web Site Not Found" came back the reply. They tried to send a thank-you email to the airline, but the email returned undeliverable. Niki dialed the phone number on the receipt. No such number. Finally, Hannah called the Amsterdam Airport and asked to be connected to the airline.

"Miss, I don't know what you are talking about. There is no such Trumpet Airline here. And such a silly name. You must be mistaken!"

The girls eyes grew big, and they looked at the Trumpet Air dolls again.

"Oh, my God!" said Niki.

Dolls in hand, they ran down the stairs. "Grandma! Mrs. Boyce! Grandma!!" exclaimed the girls. "There is no Trumpet Air! There is no Trumpet Air!"

Chapter 12
Letter from Hannah

Dear Niki,
Did you ever catch up in school after our Florence trip?

I am still scrambling. After all that happened, it is hard to concentrate. I can't believe that Brian is gone. My brother is still in shock, and so am I. My friend Ellen's uncle was killed in the World Trade Center. She thinks she can see him in one of the pictures, trapped on a ledge before the building collapsed. I wish I could do something to help her. It is so sad.

*We've done a fundraiser at school, but nothing
seems like enough. I wrote to everyone about
those poor stranded people in Europe, but I
haven't heard back from anyone. I guess
compared to being trapped in the World Trade
Center, it is not a big deal.*

*Your Aunt Mel just stopped by on her way to
Afghanistan. I can't believe she is going over
there to cover that slimy war. Grandma told me
to write you in snail mail because this
information should not go out online. I'm
staying at her house for the weekend.*

*Mel called her sources, and there is no Trumpet
Airlines! So like, are we in the* X-Files *land
or what? Anyway, she said that some Italian
guy connected to organized crime secretly
chartered the flight to get his mother back to the
U.S. before President Bush started bombing
Afghanistan.*

*He paid off that ticket agent/flight attendant
to manage it. That's why she was both ticket
agent and flight attendant! It's all hush-hush*

with no paper trail. One of Aunt Mel's newspaper buddies was on our flight, and he investigated it when he got back. It was those retro outfits that made him suspicious. He travels all over, and he said he would have remembered that get-up. So we were saved by organized crime! Those outfits were from a Milan dinner show!

Tony was moved to a Michigan jail. So was that other creep they arrested who was supposed to be part of the attack but was arrested for taking flying lessons where he only wanted to fly and not take off or land. They are charging Tony with smuggling for now, but they confiscated his laptop and searched his office in Florence.

Turns out his name is not Vasari. He is originally from Saudi Arabia! Creep. I still get hysterical laughing thinking of all of us in the dorm slapping Tony. I guess it was wrong, but it felt soooo good! Anyway, we got to hit one terrorist for all those poor people who died.

I am so glad that Kathy and her parents made it out of that plane crash alive. The Italian police arrested a suspect who checked luggage and didn't get on. The bomb malfunctioned on take off so the plane crashed, but no one was killed. Scary.

My dad was all ticked off at my mom for being in the World Trade Center during the bombing. Like she knew it was going to happen! I am starting to see what a pain he was to be married to. I still wish they weren't divorced, though. I don't know what is wrong with me. You are so lucky that your parents are still married. I'm happy for you.

At first, Daddy said that I could never fly anywhere again, but I reminded him he bought our tickets for the leadership conference at the new aquarium on Maui already. He backed down, since he set it up, and I can't wait to go with you! It will look great on our college applications, and let's face it—Maui!

I called Mom. I am so glad that she didn't die in the World Trade Center. I am going to try to be nicer. She said she was on the thirty-fifth floor. Once the first plane hit, she ran out and caught a ferry to New Jersey. She still loves teaching at Columbia in New York City and is staying there.

Well, gotta go. Miss ya. Write soon!

Love ya,

Hannah

Bibliography

1. Lewis, Bernard. *What Went Wrong?*. New York: Oxford University Press, 2002.

2. Ahmed, Akbar S. *Islam Today*. New York: I.B. Tauris Publishers, 1999, 2001.

3. Ambrose, Stephen E. *The Good Fight*. New York: Atheneum Books, 2001.

4. Sepia Studio Redazionale. *Florence for Teens*. Florence, Italy: Welcome Books, 2001.

5. Tarchi, Rossella. *The Rediscovery of the Last Judgment*. Florence, Italy: Santa Maria del Fiore, 1997.

6. "Diamonds: The Real Story," by Andrew Cockburn, *National Geographic*, 201:3, March, 2002, pp.2-35.

7. Casa Editrice Bonechi. *Florence – All of the City and Its Masterpieces*. Florence, Italy: Casa Editrice Bonechi.

8. Franchi, Mario. *Santa Croce*. Florence, Italy: Becocci.

9. Di Cagno, Gabriella. *The Cathedral.* Florence, Italy: Edizioni Mandragora, 2000.

10. Catling, Christopher. *Florence and Tuscany.* New York: Dorling Kindersley, 1994, 2000.

11. Hammond, Inc. *Atlas of the Middle East.* Union, NJ: Hammond World Atlas Corporation, 2001.

12. Montresor, Carlo. *The Opera del Duomo Museum in Florence.* Florence, Italy: Mandragora, 2000.

13. Bonsanti, Giorgio. *The Galleria della Accademia.* Florence, Italy: Editrice Giusti di Becocci, 1987.

14. Cesati, Franco. *The Medici.* Florence, Italy: La Mandragora, 1999.

15. Canali, Ferruccio. *The Basilica of Santa Croce.* Florence, Italy: Bonechi – Edizioni "Il Turismo".

16. Stopani, Romato. *Art and History of Florence.* Florence, Italy: Casa Editrice Bonechi.

17. Muccini, Ugo, Cecchi, Alessandro. *The Apartments of Cosimo in Palazzo Vecchio.* Florence, Italy: Casa Editrice La Lettere, 1991.

18. Shangle, Barbara. *Day of Terror.* Beaverton, Oregon: American Products Publishing Company, 2001.

ABOUT THE AUTHORS

The Hannah and Niki Adventures™ series inspire girls to think, be brave, and live life to the fullest while learning about history and cool places to visit. Jean and Linda look forward to exploring the world with Hannah and Niki and sharing their exciting adventures with you. To purchase additional copies of this book, visit the InfoHi Book Store at www.infohi.com or call 831-685-1063.